Because Of Your Love

ANITA SHARMA

Because Of Your Love
Copyright © 2020 by Anita Sharma

All rights reserved. No part of this publication may be reproduced, distributed, or transmitted in any form or by any means, including photocopying, recording, or other electronic or mechanical methods, without the prior written permission of the author, except in the case of brief quotations embodied in critical reviews and certain other non-commercial uses permitted by copyright law.

Tellwell Talent
www.tellwell.ca

ISBN
978-0-2288-3890-6 (Paperback)
978-0-2288-3891-3 (eBook)

*For my parents and
my husband.*

One

She was sitting on the porch, her eyes were on the road, checking every car passing by. A women's magazine was resting on her lap, but she had hardly turned a page. She always looked forward to these visits and today she had been waiting anxiously from early morning.

She had no idea how long she had been sitting here. She had finished two cups of tea. It was peaceful and quiet except for the few cars passing by. One could only hear light splashes of water on the rocks and a slow breeze through the tree leaves. Though it was past noon, the sun was still high in the sky. It felt warm and nice.

It was the end of the year, December, when everyone was in a holiday mood. Normally when one hears 'December' they think of the cold and imagine the snowflakes, but it was the opposite down under. It's the place where one can enjoy Christmas in a bikini by the beach, as it is summer, and the weather is impeccable.

She reached for her phone, thinking of making a call to ask for the reason for the delay, when a familiar car pulled up in her driveway. Her face lightened up instantly. She put aside her phone on a small table beside her where tea mugs were resting and started waving in excitement.

When the car stopped, the rear door opened first and out jumped a young girl with brown hair falling over her shoulders.

"Nana!" she cried, as she rushed towards the house.

Mia had just turned twelve and was growing more beautiful with each passing year. She threw her arms around her grandmother, hugging her tightly. Maya hugged her, ran her fingers through her soft hair, and then pulled her away. She cupped her little face in her hands.

"Look at you, such a pretty face," she said, kissing her forehead.

Mia beamed and giggled. "I missed you, nana," she said.

"I missed you too, my darling," Maya replied softly.

"Nana, nana!" cried Josh. His mom was helping him get out of the car. He ran as fast as he could, hugged Maya and asked in a cheerful voice, "Can we go fishing, nana?"

Josh was eight years old and he loved fishing trips. His dad took him along whenever he went fishing. Since his grandmother lived near a bay, Josh was always excited about these visits, as he could go fishing all day.

"Yes, Josh. Later maybe," Maya replied, with a smile. She adored her grandson.

"Why not now?" Josh questioned, with surprise. He seemed to be disappointed.

"You have to wait for your dad, remember?" Ruby was walking towards her mother. She ruffled her fingers through Josh's hair. "Hey, mom!" She leaned down and kissed her mother on her cheeks.

"You look lovely, darling," Maya said, admiring her daughter.

"And you look beautiful, mom. How you doing?" Ruby observed her mother closely.

Maya smiled and waved her hand. "I'm doing good. How was the drive? Are you tired?" she asked.

"It was okay, we made a few stops to stretch," Ruby replied.

"Where is Mike?" Maya asked. She hadn't seen him in the car when they arrived.

"He got off at the city center to catch up with his mate," Ruby explained. "I'll go and pick him up later."

It was only a few minutes' drive to the city from where Maya lived.

Josh was getting bored with the adult conversation so he asked his mum if he could play a game on his tablet. When Ruby said he could, he went inside the house.

Mia was busy on her mobile. She had found herself a chair and was sitting with her legs crossed. Her fingers were busy typing with a speed that amazed her grandmother.

"Kids these days!" Maya said, looking at her granddaughter.

"Kids?" said Ruby, "Everyone is like that nowadays. You have to see us at home. Josh is busy playing games on his tablet. Mia is like that with her headphones plugged in. Mike is either on his laptop or his phone doing his work. If he doesn't have any work to do, he is busy watching funny videos on YouTube."

Maya was amused. "What do you do then?" she asked.

"I watch television or check my phone. Then I get bored and yell at Mike, saying he is not being a good father or a good husband," Ruby said.

"Does that help?" Maya asked.

"For a while, yes." Ruby continued, "He puts down his phone and pulls me towards him, then asks me how my day was. I tell him what I did throughout the day. And then he is back on his phone again."

"Then what do you do?" Maya was finding it interesting.

"I go back to my phone," Ruby grinned.

Maya smiled and shook her head, "They say phones were invented to connect people, you know." Then they both laughed.

"The weather here is a beauty," Ruby said, stretching her legs in front of her. She had found another chair.

"It must be hot in Perth," Maya said, remembering her days there.

"It's going to be around forty degrees for five straight days," Ruby complained, rolling her eyes. "I'm glad we are here."

It's scorching hot during December and January in Perth. Temperature rises to forty degrees and above. It is cooler in Albany which is south of Perth. Most people drive down south for their Christmas and New Year's holidays to escape the heat. It is a beautiful place with lovely beaches to relax. The holiday houses, caravan parks and hotels are packed with visitors at this time of the year.

"Do you remember our holidays here when you were little?" Maya asked her daughter.

"Oh yes, I do," Ruby smiled. "I always loved camping. I found it very exciting to sleep in a tent under the open sky."

"Once, we were planning to book a holiday house, but you insisted on camping. You even said that you wouldn't go if you had to sleep in a house. Uncle David had to set up the tents in the backyard whenever we stayed here in his house," Maya said, laughing lightly.

Ruby laughed too and was about to say something when her phone beeped. She scanned through it and said, "Oh well, good for me."

"What is it?" Maya asked.

"It's Mike, he says his mate will drop him, so I don't have to drive anymore." She looked relaxed. "I'll check on Josh." She headed inside the house and murmured, "It smells nice in here!"

Two

Mia was still busy on her phone. She had pulled her legs up and was resting the phone on her knees. She read something on her phone, smiled and started to type again. She looked like her mom when she smiled. Her eyes lightened up just like Ruby's, but they were blue like her dad's. It felt like yesterday when Maya had held Mia in her arms for the first time.

She was a bundle of joy for all of them. Ruby and Mike were able to have her after a few IVF treatments. They had tried many times and after a few tests they had come to know that they could have a baby only after the treatment. They were stressed and anxious, but it was all worth it when they had Mia.

Maya observed her granddaughter carefully. As she was smiling and typing, her cheeks flushed lightly.

"Special friend?" Maya asked, with a smile.

Mia was startled by her grandmother's question. Her eyes met Maya's gaze and she blushed even more. Maya was eying her closely. She raised her brows and smiled.

Mia was close to her nana; she shared her experiences with her. If something interesting happened, she would call Maya and give her all the details. Maya loved to hear her gossips.

Mia pulled her chair closer to her grandmother.

"He is so cute, nana," she sounded dreamy.

Now it was Maya who was startled. "What do you mean? You were chatting with a boy?"

"Of course," Mia giggled, "What were you thinking?"

"I mean, aren't you too young for that?"

Mia shrugged. "Oh nana! It's nothing like that." Mia went on to explain, "Alex is a boy in my class. He is very nice and sweet and cute. And he is a very good friend of mine. He has gone to Sydney for holidays with his family. He was saying that he was having a good time."

"By the look on your face I can tell that you really like him," Maya smiled, "But being your nana, I would say it's too early for you to be falling for any boy."

"How early nana? I mean when will it be the right time for me and how will I know?" Mia asked in one breath.

"My word, you are a curious girl," Maya said. "You will know when the right time comes and when you will meet the right one for you, dear. For now, you need to focus on your studies."

"Will I know he is the right one for me as soon as I meet him?" Mia was throwing one question after the other at Maya; she wouldn't stop.

"I can't say for sure, darling," Maya went on, "Some say they fell in love at first sight. They knew the moment they met for the first time that they were meant for each other. But I couldn't understand how one could decide about their life in one meeting or even in one gaze. You can't tell how the person actually is by just looking at them…"

Mia was struggling to catch up with what her nana was saying. "Did you know it, when you met grandpa?" she interrupted.

Maya was surprised by the question. She thought for some time, and then said, "No dear, it wasn't a love at first sight. We took our time…"

"Did you like him, in the beginning?" Mia interrupted her again.

"Yes, I did, he was a nice man. But it took me sometime to know him better," Maya said, gazing towards the horizon.

Mia would have asked another question if it wasn't for Josh.

"Mia, Mia!" Little Josh rushed towards them. He was holding a football and was breathing heavily. He had been playing in the backyard.

It was a single-story house, with three bedrooms and was close to the bay. There was a small porch to one side of the entrance with timber floorboards. Maya spent most of her time sitting on the porch, reading while sipping her tea. She had interest in knitting too, but now it was a bit of an effort for her. Although she was just fifty-nine, she would strain her back easily.

The house had a backyard where there was a barbeque grill and a patio with a six-seater dining table. A white fence went around the house with a small gate at the end of the driveway. There wasn't a garage, so either the driveway or the side of the road was used for parking.

Within a few minutes' walk there was a bay, where one could see some men on the rocks with their fishing rods in the evening. Some would be seen swimming in the shallow, clear water. There was a small café nearby which was busy most of the time during the holidays.

"Let's go and play!" Josh was pulling his sister by her hand.

Mia wanted to stay with her grandmother and talk some more but Josh was almost begging her to play with him; she couldn't say no to him.

"Let's go," she said, getting up, and then she went with him.

Maya smiled at them as she watched them go towards the backyard. She was glad that they got along so well.

It was quiet again. Maya thought about going inside the house too. But then she decided to stay a bit longer and watch the sun descend. It always looked beautiful as the sky changed its color, and it would remind her of the sunsets she used to watch.

She smiled as she thought of her talk with Mia and began to ponder upon Mia's question. Thinking about the answer, her thoughts wandered into the past and all the memories came flooding back.

Three

Maya was her parents' only child. They lived in Perth, in a small house which was about twenty minutes' walk from the city center. They did not have a car, so walking was the only option for them to get to the city or the markets. Maya could hardly remember going out anywhere except her school and places where her mother, Jane, worked. Her father had taken her to the beach once when she was small. She had loved playing in the sand. Her father had held her hands as she splashed in the waves. She had expected and wanted to go to the beach again, but that never happened.

Her father worked in a local bar serving beer to the customers. Most of the nights he would come home drunk and go to bed straight away. After waiting for him throughout the evening, Maya and her mother had to eat dinner without him. Sometimes, he would come home sober and they would have dinner together. After dinner, he would go to his room with a book or a newspaper and close the door behind him.

There were no family talks or chats or laughter in the house; it was mostly quiet. After doing the dishes and cleaning the kitchen, Jane would sit with her and ask about her school. Jane would help Maya with her schoolwork, and make sure that she understood what she learned.

Often Jane talked about people at her work, or anything interesting that had happened throughout the day. Maya loved listening to her mother's stories. She was very good at telling them; she made normal situations sound dramatic.

Jane worked in a bakery nearby, from Monday to Saturday. On Sunday and Thursday evenings she worked at Mr. and Mrs. Smiths' house.

Maya went to the bakery on Saturdays with her mother. Jane worked by the oven, putting in dough and pulling out breads when they were ready. The room would be very hot during summers, making it worse for Jane to work there, but she never complained. She made sure that Maya was out at the counter with Sally, who was a cheerful lady and chatted nonstop. She liked Maya and often said that she was very quiet for her age.

On Sunday and Thursday evenings, Maya would go with Jane to the Smiths' house. It was the biggest house she had ever seen. There were so many rooms that Maya thought she would get lost if she wandered alone in there. There was a television in the living area, a beautiful chandelier hanging from the ceiling, paintings and family photos scattered on the wall. The kitchen was huge with white tiles and utensils that she had never seen.

It was a treat for her to come here. She could have juice in summer and hot chocolate in winter. Sometimes she would be lucky and get cakes and sweets. Mrs. Smith was a nice lady; she was always gentle with Maya.

Mr. and Mrs. Smith had three kids, one girl and twin boys. Sophie was the same age as Maya and the twins were younger. Maya used to play with Sophie. Mrs. Smith was glad that her daughter had company.

"They get along so well," she often used to say.

While Maya would be enjoying herself, Jane would be busy cleaning the house. She did the laundry: washed the clothes, dried, and ironed them. She then hanged or folded them neatly and stacked them in place. She cleaned the kitchen and the dishes until they sparkled like new. She wiped the windows, mopped the floors, and dusted the rest of the house.

Sometimes she had to prepare lunch or dinner as well. If Mr. and Mrs. Smith went out for some function, she had to babysit the little ones. Sophie would play with Maya, but the twins could be a handful, making her very tired after the day's work.

Whenever the Smiths went to the beach on a Sunday, they would invite Maya too. It was exciting for her to ride in their car. The kids would play in the sand, making sandcastles. Mr. and Mrs. Smith would lay nearby watching their kids, talking and laughing. They looked so happy together, Maya thought, even as a kid. When they kissed, Maya would feel shy and look away. She wondered why her parents never kissed or laughed together or even talked to one another.

One evening, Jane told Maya that she had to babysit at the Smiths' as they were going out for dinner. As soon as they entered the house, Mrs. Smith dragged Jane into her room, saying she couldn't decide what to wear for the night. Sophie was playing with her dolls in the living room. Maya went towards Sophie and started to play with her. Mr. Smith was with the twins. He was wearing a black suit and looked very handsome.

After a while, he went to knock on the door to the room where Mrs. Smith had vanished with Jane. "Are you ready yet?" he asked.

"Almost done, darling," came Mrs. Smith's frantic voice from inside.

The door opened almost half an hour later and out stepped Mrs. Smith wearing a long red dress and sparkling earrings. Her shoulder length golden brown hair was hanging on one side. With red lips and black eye shadow, she looked very beautiful.

Mr. Smith was staring at his wife with his mouth half open. "Wow! You look lovely, my darling," he said. He was admiring her.

Mrs. Smith smiled and walked gracefully with her man out the door.

"She looks so pretty, mom," Maya said.

"She is pretty," Jane replied with a smile.

Jane fed the twins a bottle of milk each and changed them. After some struggle, Jane was able to put the twins to sleep. By that time, the girls were yawning. Jane took Sophie to her room and tucked her into her bed. She stroked her hair gently until she fell asleep.

When she went to the living room, Maya was curled up on the couch, fast asleep. Jane sat beside her and patted her head gently. Jane was very tired; her eyelids were feeling heavy. She was trying hard not to fall asleep but in vain. She was snoring lightly in no time.

A soft knock on the front door woke her up. She had no idea how long she had been asleep for. She went to the door to open it. Mrs. Smith walked in with a big smile on her face.

"He is waiting in the car to drop you home," she said, in a low voice.

"Did you have a lovely time?" Jane asked.

"Oh yes, dear, it was lovely," Mrs. Smith replied. "Did you have much trouble with the kids?"

"Not at all, they are angels." She then remembered that Mr. Smith was waiting in the car. "We should be going now," she said, then woke Maya gently. "Let's go home, sweetie."

"Thank you so much for looking after the kids," Mrs. Smith said.

Maya was yawning and rubbing her eyes. She was half asleep while her mother led her away. They walked towards the car, the engine was still running.

"Sorry to keep you waiting," Jane apologized to Mr. Smith, as she helped Maya into the backseat and climbed in beside her.

"It's okay, Jane, and thank you for tonight," he said softly.

They drove quietly towards Jane's house which was not far away. When the car stopped in front of her house, Jane got off and helped Maya out of the car.

"Thank you," Jane said, looking towards Mr. Smith. He lowered his head a little with a smile and drove off.

Jane and Maya hurried towards the door; it was unlocked. They entered slowly. Jane took Maya to her room and put her to bed. After tucking the blanket around her, she kissed her forehead.

"Good night, darling," she whispered.

Maya did not answer, she was asleep already and breathing heavily. Jane walked out of her room quietly.

Maya stirred in her sleep; she could hear voices in her dream. The voices grew louder, and she woke up, but she could still hear them. She sat upright in her bed and tried to clear her head. It was her parents' voices that she was hearing. They seemed to be arguing. She couldn't make out what they were saying, but her dad was yelling. A little later she heard the front door open and then shut with a loud bang.

She waited for some time then crept out of her bed, walked to her mother's room slowly and peeked inside through the door. Jane was sitting at the end of her bed, looking down at her hands that were resting on her laps.

"Mommy," Maya said, in a small voice.

Jane looked up at her with sad eyes, tears were rolling down her cheeks. She opened her arms and nodded her head.

Maya walked into her arms. "What's wrong, mommy?" she asked, in a shaky voice.

Jane held her tight, wiped her tears and kissed her little girl on her head. "Nothing, darling, daddy was a little upset because mommy was late and dinner was not ready," Jane said to her daughter. "You go to sleep, love; it's very late."

"I am scared, mommy." Maya sounded like she was about to cry.

Jane's heart ached to see her like that. "Sleep with mommy," she said, as she stroked her hair.

Maya looked relieved and climbed on her mother's bed. Jane covered her with a blanket and sat beside her, resting her back on a pillow.

"Good night, mommy." Maya was already feeling better.

"Good night, darling." Jane patted her head slowly with one hand. She knew it was going to be a long night. She just sat on her bed staring at the wall in front of her.

Four

Growing up, Maya realized that her parents were not on good terms with one another, there was no love between them. After that night, her father had returned home two days later. He didn't explain where he had been, he didn't even say a single word to either of them. She wanted to play with him, talk with him and hug him, but his stiff figure and stern face stopped her from doing so. The silence and distance grew even more in the following days.

The environment at home had made her quiet and reserved. She didn't talk much, even with her friends at school. She was a smart kid, but something held her back. Jane had noticed that her daughter was very quiet unlike other kids of her age. She tried to start conversations with her all the time. Maya seemed to be interested, but all she did was smile and nod her head.

She had a very good imagination though and sometimes she would talk to herself. She would imagine two different characters and start a conversation between them. Her mother had seen her do it a few times. At first she was worried, but later she thought, at least she is talking.

Maya was interested in one thing: watching stars at night. Most of the nights when the sky was clear and stars were twinkling, she would go at the back of the house and sit on the stairs, staring at the sky. Sometimes, she would try to count the stars, and sometimes she would imagine gliding through them or jumping from one star to another. She thought the stars were her friends and often talked to them. She shared her feelings and her opinions on different things. At times, she even made wishes, and in her wish, she asked for a happy life for her and her mom.

Maya liked going to the bakery with her mom because she could see Sally, who always seemed to be happy. She smiled all the time and chatted with her customers. Maya would giggle when she talked to her with funny voices and expressions. Sally used to knit whenever she had time at work. When there were no customers, she would sit on a chair and pull out her knitting needles and yarn. It amazed Maya to see how fast her fingers moved with the needles. She could even knit without looking at her work.

Sally had noticed that Maya was interested in what she was doing. "You wanna try?" she asked her.

Maya nodded.

"Here, give it a go," Sally said, handing over the needles to Maya.

The needles were big for her little fingers, but she managed to hold them.

"Hold them like this," Sally said, as she helped her. "Now put the right needle through this loop on the left needle, wrap the yarn around it and pull it through the loop. Now let the loop go off the left needle like this."

Sally made it look so easy, but Maya was struggling to understand what she had just watched. Sally smiled and showed it to her again slowly. Maya concentrated and tried herself and managed to knit a stitch. She was so excited that she was beaming.

"See you got it. You are a smart kid." Sally patted her shoulder. Maya grinned even more.

"Now go on and finish the row for me," Sally said, and went on to serve her customer who had just arrived at the counter.

Maya went slow and steady focusing on her work like it was very important to her. She managed to finish the row after some time. When her mom came to get her to go home, she shouted with excitement, "Mommy, see! I helped Sally to knit!"

Jane looked at Sally who said, "Yes, she has done a great job, look at this." She showed the knit work to Jane.

Jane was overwhelmed to see Maya so happy. She turned to her and with a surprise look on her face she said, "You really did that by yourself, darling?"

Maya nodded proudly.

"Even I can't knit, you are very smart." She then turned to Sally. "Thank you," she said, her eyes were moist.

Sally squeezed her hand and smiled with a nod, then looked at Maya and said, "Next time when you are here, I'll let you do some more and later I'll teach you how to do patterns."

Maya clapped her hands with joy. She had a wide grin on her face all the way home. She couldn't wait to see Sally again. From then onwards, she never missed a single visit to the bakery.

One evening, Maya and Jane were waiting as usual for her father to come home for dinner. It was a few months past Maya's thirteenth birthday. It was getting late and Maya was hungry, but he didn't show up. Jane told Maya to have her dinner while she waited a bit longer. After finishing her dinner, Maya went to her room. She had no idea how long her mom had been up waiting for her father. In the morning, she found out that he had not come home at all.

The next day, they waited again, but he didn't turn up that day either. The following day, they didn't wait for him. They had their dinner and left the food for him on the table. There was no sign of him the next morning, and the food was untouched. They had no idea why he wasn't home for almost a week. Jane even stopped making dinner for him, and they didn't wait for him anymore.

Maya was at the bakery again, learning some new patterns with Sally. So far, she had helped Sally finish a shawl with simple knits.

A heavily built man walked up to the counter.

"What can I get ya?" Sally asked, in her usual cheerful voice with a big smile on her face.

"I am her to see Jane," the man said, in a deep voice.

Hearing her mom's name, Maya looked up at him, but could not recognize him from anywhere.

Without further question, Sally went into the back of the bakery to inform Jane.

"Yes, how can I help you?" Jane asked the man as she walked out. Maya could tell that even her mom did not recognize him.

"I work in the same bar as your husband," the man said to Jane.

The smile on Jane's face faded away. She signaled the man and they both went to a corner. They talked for some time. Maya could see that the man was shaking his head and her mom was looking down with her hands covering her mouth. Then the man patted Jane gently on her shoulder and left.

Jane turned around, walked towards her daughter and hugged her. She had tears in her eyes. She shut them in anguish. There was a mixture of emotions: sadness, anger, distress, and even some relief.

"Is everything all right, Jane?" Sally was concerned. "What did he say?"

Wiping her tears, Jane went on to explain that the man worked with her husband in the bar. He had come to question about him as he was missing from work for more than a week without any notice. The man also told her that her husband often talked about the ships in Fremantle harbor. A couple of times, they had even visited the harbor together. Once he had said that he wanted to get on one of those ships, sail around the world and never come back. The man assumed that he might have done it after all.

Jane eyes were red with anger. Maya started to cry too, seeing her mother in tears.

"I'm so sorry, Jane." Sally hugged them both. She couldn't say anything more.

Back home, Maya noticed that her mom was quiet, lost in her own thoughts most of the time, for the next few days. She couldn't understand why her father had left them. Was she not a good daughter? Hadn't her mom done enough for him, for his family? How could he be so selfish and heartless? She thought, in anger. She started to hate her father for making her mom sad.

A few days later, one night after dinner, Jane walked into Maya's room and sat on her bed next to her. She held her daughter's hand and looked into her eyes.

"Just because he left us doesn't mean we have to live our lives in sadness," Jane said, in a low voice. "We don't need him to be happy. We have each other and that is enough for us. And that is what we are going to do from now on, be happy, okay, sweetie?" More than a request, it sounded like a promise to her daughter.

"Okay." Maya nodded her head in agreement.

Five

Things started to get back to normal around the house in the following days. Maya had been worried for her mom after her father had left. To her surprise, Jane seemed to be much more relaxed and content. Seeing her mother like that made her happy too. There were no more arguments, no more sad faces, no more waiting at the dinner table, and Maya preferred it that way.

Jane had found herself a new job at a café in the city. She had to work extra now. She continued to work at the Smiths' twice a week. On her next visit to the Smiths' after her father's disappearance, Maya had felt a bit uncomfortable.

"You poor little thing!" Mrs. Smith had said, when she saw Maya. The sympathy was obvious when she hugged Jane. "What are you going to do?" she had said.

But Maya did not appreciate it, she did not want people to have pity on them.

Maya slowly limited her visits to the Smiths', and then stopped altogether. She would rather go to the bakery and spend time with Sally. Most of the time, she would be at home all by herself. She cleaned the house and prepared dinner when her mom was working late. While working in the house, she would pretend that she had company. She would imagine having visitors and talk with herself. Most of the time, she didn't even realize that she was doing it.

On her sixteenth birthday, Jane handed her a giftbag. She hugged her tight, kissed her on her forehead, and said, "Happy birthday, darling!"

"What is it, mom?" Maya took the bag with a big smile.

"Have a look yourself." Jane was happy to see her excited.

Maya opened the bag and pulled out two balls of yarn. They were soft and bright red in color. At the bottom were a pair of knitting needles.

Maya was overjoyed, "Thanks, mom!" She gave her a tight hug.

She couldn't wait to start a project with it but needed help from Sally. She had made up her mind about what she was going to make. She went to see Sally a few days later when her mom was working in the café. She did not want her mom to know what she was going to knit. Sally was more than eager to help her with the project.

"What a brilliant idea!" She said when Maya told her about her little plan.

Once a week, Maya would go to the Swan River, which was about thirty minutes' walk from her house. She found it refreshing to walk along the bank of the river, especially during hot weather. The cool breeze would wash down the temperature. She would find a spot on the grass and sit down, stretching her legs in front of her. She enjoyed watching the seagulls flying over the water, searching for food to eat.

A few couples would walk by, holding hands, looking very happy together. They made her wonder if she would ever walk along the riverbank or the beach holding someone's hand. Would she ever find someone who would love her?

The memory of Mr. and Mrs. Smith being romantic on the beach would flash in her mind. She would wonder what it would feel like to be kissed or to kiss someone. A warm sensation would creep up her body when she had such thoughts.

Maya had finished her knitting project and was very happy with the outcome. One night after dinner, she told her mother she had something for her.

"What is it, love?" Jane asked, as she had no clue.

"You will see in a bit, mom." Maya went to her room and came back with her hands behind her.

"Close your eyes," she said in excitement.

Jane smiled and did as she was told.

Maya wrapped a red scarf around Jane's neck and adjusted it. "Open your eyes."

Jane touched the woolen scarf and looked down at it. She unwrapped it from her neck and looked at it more carefully running her hand along it. It was a wide, bright red scarf with big cable stitches and looked beautiful.

Jane's eyes moistened, and with a wide grin, she hugged her daughter. "It's lovely, thank you, darling. I can't wait for winter," she said, and wrapped it around again. Though it was warm in the house, she did not take it off until she went to bed.

Maya was very happy that her mom liked it so much.

A month went by in a usual routine until one evening, when Jane returned home late from the Smiths'. She kept mumbling and shaking her head as if in disbelief.

"Oh, good lord, how could she?" Maya caught her mom saying out loud.

"Are you okay, mom?" She was concerned.

"She is too young." Jane was shaking her head again.

Maya was confused. She couldn't make out what was bothering her mom so much. She held Jane's arm and shook her a bit. "Will you tell me what's the matter?"

Jane seemed to be woken up from sleep. "Sophie," was all she could say.

"What about her?" Maya asked.

"Sophie is pregnant!" Jane blurted out.

"What?" Maya covered her mouth in disbelief.

"She is just sixteen. How could she be so stupid and careless?" Jane said.

"Mom," Maya tried to say something, but Jane continued to talk.

"She should have cared for her parents. Mr. Smith is angry but quiet. Mrs. Smith can't stop wailing. They can't figure out what to do next. It's complete chaos in the house." She was waving her hands in the air.

"How is Sophie?" Maya asked as she was worried about her.

"She has locked herself in her room." Jane shook her head, then turned to Maya. Looking deep into her eyes, she said to her, "Promise me one thing, Maya. You won't do anything stupid like that."

Maya was taken aback by what her mom had just said to her. Weren't they talking about Sophie?

Jane was holding her arms now, "Look, Maya. You are young and beautiful. Men will ask you out."

No, they won't, Maya thought.

"I don't want you to date anyone unless you know him well," her mother continued, "And no fooling around. You have to be careful and sensible."

Maya didn't know how to respond to her mom.

Later as she sat on her bed, Maya kept thinking about Sophie and what her mom had said to her earlier. Her mom was worrying for no reason, she thought. She wasn't pretty like Sophie and no man was going to find her attractive or take her on a date, ever.

Maya wanted to meet up with Sophie and see how she was doing. The next day, she went to the Smiths' with Jane. Avoiding the elders, she went straight to Sophie's room and knocked on the door. There was no reply. She knocked again and said, "Sophie are you in there? It's Maya."

"Come in," said an anxious voice.

Maya slowly opened the door and stepped inside. Sophie jumped from her bed and hugged Maya.

"Oh, Maya, I am so glad to see you," she said in a hoarse voice. Her eyes were red and puffed, and her hair was tangled and frizzy.

"How are you doing?" Maya asked her.

"I don't know," Sophie started to sob again. "Dad doesn't talk to me, mom is crying all the time. I don't know what to do."

"You need to get a hold of yourself, look at you." Maya tried to smooth out her hair. "You want to tell me about him?"

"His name is George," Sophie said, "We went to the same school; he is a few years senior and we have been seeing each other for six months now. He is a nice man, you know."

"Have you two talked about this?" Maya asked.

"I haven't met him after I knew about it." Sophie cracked again. "My parents haven't allowed me to go out of the house."

"Crying won't help, Sophie. You need to meet George soon and talk about what you should do next. Tell your parents that you have to see him." Maya sounded firm, but Sophie looked nervous.

"Take it easy; everything will be okay," Maya said as she hugged Sophie, who smiled for the first time in days. She relaxed her tensed shoulders. She was glad that Maya had come to see her.

Six

Maya had prepared dinner and was waiting for her mother to be home from the Smiths'. She wondered how things were going on with Sophie. It had been a couple of days after she had seen her. Jane came home a bit late, and she was exhausted.

"I'm home!" she said loudly.

"Dinner is ready, mom," Maya said from the kitchen.

Jane sat down for dinner. She hadn't cared to change her clothes or wash her hands. While eating, Maya studied her mom. For the first time, she realized that her mother was growing old. She could see the fine lines at the corner of her eyes and lips, and dark circles under her eyes. She seemed to have lost some weight too. Maya thought it was because of the hard work she did.

"Mom, you need to slow down," Maya said.

"What?" Jane was startled. She looked down at her plate. "Am I eating too fast?" she asked.

"I did not mean your food. I mean you need to slow down with your work," Maya said.

"What do you mean?" Jane looked up from her plate and stared at her daughter. "We need money to survive and I need to work for that money."

"I know we need the money, mom, but you don't have to work so hard. I should start working too," Maya said.

"But, Maya," Jane was about to say something, but Maya interrupted her.

"Mom, I am old enough to work and I have decided that I will start looking for a job. You have been working too much for too long."

"I don't reckon that's a good idea. You need to complete your studies first, it's important," Jane said.

"You are more important to me, mom. Let me help you. Besides, I don't enjoy school much," Maya said.

Jane thought for some time and then smiled. "I could talk with Wendy, if you want." Wendy was the owner of the café where she worked.

"That would be great," Maya said.

"It will be fun working together, you and I." Jane got up, picked up her plate and walked towards the sink.

"No, mom. You are not working at the café anymore," Maya was stern.

Jane stopped midway and turned around to look at her daughter.

"You can work at the bakery and at the Smiths' if you want, but no more than that. I am replacing you at the café." Maya stood up and started clearing the table.

Jane did not know how to react to what her daughter had said, she just continued to stare at her. Her little girl was all grown up now, and she had grown into a beautiful lady. She was tall and slender with pale skin. Her hair was wavy, light brown falling just below her broad shoulders.

"How are things at the Smiths', how is Sophie?' Maya asked, as she passed by Jane, walking towards the sink with her plate. Jane was still admiring her daughter.

"All going good there. Sophie talked with her man; they have decided to get married before the baby is born. They have their parents' consent to do so. Now everyone is busy planning the wedding," Jane said, as she cleaned the dishes.

"That's good," Maya said with a smile. "When is the wedding?"

"They haven't fixed the date yet, but Sophie wants it to be soon so that she won't show her baby bump and can fit into a lovely wedding dress," Jane replied.

Maya was happy for Sophie that things were going well for her.

"When the big day comes, I will be busy at their house for a few days," Jane said. "Sophie was asking for you, can you go see her tomorrow?"

"I will," Maya said, "And you don't forget to talk with Wendy tomorrow. I would like to start soon."

Maya went to meet Sophie the next day. Mrs. Smith greeted her at the door, signaling towards the backyard, she vanished into the kitchen. Maya walked towards the backyard, stealing a quick glance around the house. Nothing much had changed since her last visit.

Sophie was sitting on the patio with someone, deep in conversation and excited at the same time. When she saw Maya, she jumped off her chair and went to hold her hands.

"I am glad you could come. I've got to tell you a lot of things," she said.

Maya smiled at her.

"That's our caretaker," Sophie waved towards the man she was sitting with. "We were discussing about the decoration of the house and landscaping."

"Have you finalized the date for the wedding yet?" Maya asked her.

"Yep, we decided this morning that the wedding will be in three weeks." Sophie clapped her hands. "Thanks heaps for coming to see me when you did and talking some sense into me." Sophie held her hands again.

"No problem," Maya said softly.

"No, really. I was so scared I couldn't think straight. After talking to you, I got some courage to talk to my parents and then everything went smoothly. Though we don't have enough time for the preparation, I hope that we can pull it off." Sophie went on, "You know, I always had a dream wedding in my mind, even as a kid."

"It will be just like the way you have always wanted," Maya assured her.

They strolled around the garden for some time, Sophie explaining about the specifics she had in mind.

"Mom and I are going to a few places for the next couple of days to choose and decide on a few things like the wedding dress, flowers and cake," Sophie said, and added, "Why don't you come with us? You can help me pick the best ones."

Maya was surprised. She hadn't expected Sophie to ask for her help with the wedding preparation. After her father had left them, Maya had limited her visits to the Smiths'. She hadn't been close to Sophie after that.

"I would love to, but I am starting work from tomorrow," she blurted out, not thinking about what she was saying.

Sophie looked astounded. "What? You are working?"

"Hopefully from tomorrow," Maya said.

"Wow, okay," Sophie said, "But make sure you are free for the wedding day."

"For sure. I wouldn't miss it." Maya laughed lightly.

At home, Maya waited anxiously for her mom to return from work, hoping she hadn't forgotten to talk to the owner about her. She wished that she could start soon, even the next day wouldn't be bad. She went to the kitchen to prepare an early dinner before her mom arrived home. Dinner was almost ready when she heard the front door open.

"Mom?" she called out.

"Yes, love?" Jane replied.

"Dinner is almost ready," Maya said.

"I will take a shower first. I am all sweaty." Jane peeked into the kitchen. "Is that okay?" she asked.

"Yeah, it'll take a few more minutes," Maya replied.

Jane took a quick shower and changed into clean clothes. When she went into the kitchen, Maya was setting the table.

"Smells good," she said, sitting down.

"Chicken," Maya said with a smile and handed a plate to her mother. "How was work?" she asked.

"As usual, busy," Jane replied.

"So, did you talk about me?" She was eager to know.

Jane looked at her daughter and smiled. "Yes, I did. Wendy is more than happy to have a younger waitress than me," she said.

"When can I start?" Maya asked in excitement.

"You can come with me tomorrow. I'll show you around and you can start from the next day," Jane said through a mouthful of food.

"That will be great, thanks, mom." Maya was glad that it had worked out well. A sense of relief settled on her, thinking that her mother wouldn't be as stressed from now on.

Maya noticed that her mother was shifting her legs while doing the dishes. She asked her if she was okay. Jane said that she was a bit tired and her feet hurt a little.

Maya offered to clean the dishes and asked her to go rest in her bedroom. Later, Maya went to her room with some olive oil in a bowl. Jane was resting in her bed.

"What are you doing?" Jane was surprised.

"Giving you a foot massage." Maya grinned, sitting at the end of the bed.

"You don't have to do that. I'll be fine," Jane tried to protest but in vain.

Maya grabbed a pillow, lifted her mom's feet and rested them on the pillow. "You just sit back and relax," she said. Then she took some oil, rubbed it on her palm and started working on Jane's feet. She smoothed out the oil on her foot up to the ankle and gently rubbed from toe to heel using her thumbs. She repeated for some time and then moved onto the next foot.

Jane was enjoying the massage. The stiffness in her feet was going away. She felt relaxed and didn't realize that her eyelids were getting heavier. When she dozed off, Maya quietly left the room.

Seven

The next morning, Maya was up early. After a quick breakfast, they went to the café. There was a middle-aged woman standing behind the counter. She must have been the same age as Jane but looked younger. She wore makeup, her hair was short, and she was much heavier.

"Morning, girls. This must be Maya?" She sounded cheerful.

"Good morning, Wendy, how are you?" Jane said.

"Good, good. You are beautiful, young lady." She was admiring Maya.

"Nice to meet you, madam," Maya said with a nod.

She waved her hand. "Call me Wendy."

"I'll show her around," Jane said, leading Maya into a small room. She took two aprons hanging from the hook on the wall and handed one to Maya. Slipping them over their dresses, they walked out of the room. Jane started to set the tables and chairs.

Maya helped her mom with whatever she was doing. A few minutes later, a tall man in his mid-thirties entered the café.

"Morning, everyone!" He was loud.

Jane greeted him and introduced Maya to him. His name was Bob, and he was the cook there. After saying hello to her, he vanished behind one of the doors. A little later, people started to walk into the café for their morning coffee. Maya watched from a corner as her mother went to the tables to take the orders. She scribbled on a notepad, then went through the doors where Bob had gone earlier.

After some time, Jane walked out of the door with a tray in her hand which was loaded with three coffee cups, pies and muffins. She placed them on the table with a smile on her face. She said something to the customers which Maya couldn't hear.

More people walked into the café as the morning progressed. Jane repeated the same task and cleared the tables as the customers left. Maya could imagine how tired her mother would be at the end of the day.

After getting the hang of what her mother did or what she was supposed to do from the next day onwards, Maya thought of leaving. She took her apron off and hanged it on the same hook. She told Jane that she was leaving, then waved at Wendy.

"See you on the 'morrow," Wendy waved back.

Maya wandered around the city for another hour before heading back home.

The next morning, she got up way too early in the excitement. It was her first day at work and she didn't want to be late. She got ready, then went to the kitchen to make herself some coffee and toast. She was sipping her coffee when Jane walked in.

"You are up early," she said, scratching her head.

"Couldn't sleep." Maya shrugged.

"Excited huh?" Jane smiled. "Don't rush yourself. It's your first day so take it slow or you will tire out soon."

"Okay, mom. You have a good day." She kissed Jane on her cheek as she left.

A gush of chilled wind hit her face when she stepped out from the front door. It was the middle of July and had rained heavily all night. It was still cloudy and cold in the morning. Maya was glad that she had put on a cardigan over her blouse. She was wearing her favorite jeans and comfy shoes. Her hair was tied up in a ponytail. Even without any makeup, she looked fresh and beautiful.

She walked briskly, folding her hands across her chest to keep herself warm. Her pale cheeks started to get some color from the walk. She was rehearsing in her head how she would greet the customers and what she would say while she placed the food on their table. She was even practicing her smile, unaware of the few passersby smiling back at her.

Wendy was just opening the doors of the café when Maya arrived. "You are early, love." She grinned.

"Good morning, madam, umm, Wendy." Maya smiled. She went in to put on her apron and started to arrange the tables and chairs.

Later, Bob walked in and went to the kitchen after the greetings.

Maya hurried to a table with a notepad and a pencil as two men sat down. She greeted them with a smile and asked what they would like to have. After scribbling down the order, she went into the kitchen. She was nervous but did her best to stay calm. She handed the order to Bob and waited as he made the coffee.

When it was ready, she carried the tray carefully, hoping not to trip. She was so focused that only after placing the coffee on the table did she realize that there was another couple waiting for their order to be taken.

After a while, a man in his fifties entered the café. He smiled at Wendy and entered the kitchen. When Maya went to give another order to Bob, that man was working with him. Bob introduced them. His name was Brenton and he was another cook there.

"Hello there," he said, with a smile.

Maya smiled at him and walked out with two trays.

More people were filling the café. Wendy sensed that Maya was panicking a bit. She pulled her aside and asked her to relax. "You don't have to rush, girl; you are going good. Besides, Gloria will be here anytime," she said.

Maya blinked as she had no idea who Gloria was. Her mom hadn't mentioned her either. She continued her work, taking the orders, dropping off the food and clearing the tables. She tried to be as efficient as she could. She did not have time for a formal chat with the customers and she liked it that way.

Later, when she came out of the kitchen with loaded trays, she noticed a young lady chatting with Wendy. She was wearing a skirt and had slender long legs. She was attractive even from behind.

Wendy signaled at Maya to come over. After placing down the food, she went to the counter.

"Maya, this is Gloria, my niece," Wendy said.

"Maya, that's one interesting name," Gloria said.

Maya didn't know how to respond. She just stood there, smiling at them.

"Nice to meet ya." Gloria smiled sweetly and extended her hand towards her.

"Nice to meet you too." Maya smiled and shook her hand.

"I should get started, it's a crowd in here." Gloria went into the change room and walked out with an apron on. She winked at Maya as she walked past her towards the customers to take the orders. She greeted everyone at the table with a big smile. She kept on talking even after taking the orders. People seemed to like her. She was cheerful and was good with her small talks.

The next few hours were busy; Maya could already feel the soreness in her neck. The cloudy morning had changed into a beautiful sunny afternoon. She grabbed a sandwich and went out in the sun for her lunch break.

There were many others out and about who didn't want to miss the sun. Some were munching on their lunch and some were reading newspapers. Some were talking while enjoying the weather.

After finishing her sandwich, Maya went back to her work. Gloria was busy chatting with her customers. The café was very crowded during the lunch time, keeping everyone busy. There were fewer and fewer customers as time passed until there were only a couple left. Maya hadn't realized it was five o'clock already, time to close the café. When the last couple had finished, Maya and Gloria cleared all the tables and stacked away the chairs.

Maya went to the change room, took her apron off and put on her cardigan which she had taken off during the day. She peeked into the kitchen to say good-bye to the boys who were cleaning the dishes. Wendy and Gloria were chatting at the counter. Maya said good-bye to them.

"See ya," both said at once.

Maya walked slowly all the way home. By the time she got there, she was tired to her bones. She wanted to put her feet up and relax, but then thought a hot shower would be much better.

She took her clothes off, stepped into the shower and turned the hot water on. She stood in the shower for longer than usual, letting the hot water fall on her shoulders, easing the soreness she had there. She felt a lot better. After a few more minutes, she turned the water off, stepped out and dried herself. She changed into clean clothes, and then went into the kitchen to make some coffee.

Jane arrived home after an hour. "How was your day, darling?" she asked.

"Tiring, mom. Want some coffee? Just made it." Maya offered a cup to Jane.

"Ta," Jane said, as she took the cup and sat on the chair. "Why don't you go rest in your room? I will call you when the dinner is ready."

Maya carried her cup to the room and made herself comfortable in her bed. Savoring every sip of her coffee, she thought about the day. It hadn't been so bad, she thought. She was glad that the people she worked with were all good with her. Watching Gloria, she had learned one thing: she needed to improve her own communication skills.

Eight

The next couple of weeks were the same. Maya started at eight in the morning and worked till five in the afternoon. She had started to recognize the regulars. She smiled at everyone and looked cheerful, but her talks were limited to a "hello", "good morning" and "how are you?". Gloria, on the other hand, wouldn't miss a chance to linger at a table and talk about anything from the weather, to food, to fashion. It seemed like she knew all the details about everything.

Maya had started to like Gloria. She was sweet and kind to her. She would wink at Maya and signal with her eyes towards any young man at the café. When Maya showed no interest, she would roll her eyes. Later, when they were closing the café, she would say, "That bloke was checking you out," or "That guy was cute, wasn't he?"

Maya would just smile at her; she had come to know that she liked to have fun and didn't mind her.

Once, Maya asked her, "Why would anyone check me out and not you?" She thought Gloria was way more attractive than her.

"Because, my darling, you are a beauty," Gloria replied. "You could make anyone's head turn," she added.

Maya stared at her in disbelief. "No way," she said.

Gloria rolled her eyes again. "I'm serious."

At home, Jane reminded Maya of Sophie's wedding. "It's this coming weekend, don't forget." Jane noticed that she was a bit upset. "What's the matter?" she asked.

"I don't have anything decent to wear for the wedding," Maya complained.

Jane understood her, "How about you go shopping and get yourself a new dress?" she suggested.

Maya lightened up. She liked the idea. "Yeah, I will ask Gloria to help me buy a nice dress. She seems to know a lot about clothes."

The next day when she met Gloria, she asked her if she would help her buy a dress for a wedding party. Gloria agreed instantly and was more excited than Maya. They asked Wendy if they could be gone for an hour. Wendy said they could go only after the lunch time so that she could handle on her own.

When they went out, Gloria acted like she was on an adventure. Before Maya could stop her, Gloria dragged her into a fancy shop. There were beautiful dresses hanging on the hooks for display. Gloria started to lift them one by one and showed them to Maya, asking her what she thought about them.

"I can't afford them. Let's get out of here," she muffled.

"You don't have to buy them; we can just look around and try them," Gloria said, admiring the dresses.

"We don't have much time, let's go!" Maya was begging now.

Gloria rolled her eyes as they walked out of the store to find something less expensive. They tried a few shops until they found a lovely dress that caught their eyes. It was a beautiful yellow dress with a red floral print. Maya tried it on, and it fit her perfectly. It had no sleeves and the length was just above the knees. She liked the way she looked in it.

"Wow, it's perfect. You look lovely." Gloria grinned.

Maya paid for the dress. As they were walking out of the store, Maya noticed a pair of high heel shoes by the glass door. They would match the dress perfectly, she thought.

But after paying for the dress, she didn't have much left to spend on anything. She thought she might just have to do with her old pair of sandals.

The next day, when they were in the change room after closing the café, Gloria lifted Maya's hand and placed a yellow silk scarf on it.

Maya was surprised. "You didn't have to," she said.

"Oh, I had to. When I saw it, I thought it would match your dress," Gloria said.

"It's beautiful, thank you," Maya said, feeling the softness of the fabric. Little had she known that the scarf was going to change her life.

Jane went to the Smiths' house every day that week to help with the wedding preparations and would return home late. Knowing that her mother wouldn't be home anytime soon, Maya would stroll around the city after work. She would go to the Swan River and walk along the bank or sit on a bench and observe her surroundings.

On the wedding day, Jane left for the Smiths' early in the morning. "Don't be late," she said to Maya before she left.

"Okay, mom." Maya pulled the cover over her head. She was still in bed and had no plans to hurry. She slept till late in the morning. When she finally got up from the bed, it was half past ten. She took her time to finish a cup of coffee. The weather looked perfect for the wedding day.

Thinking she should better start getting ready for the wedding, she went for a quick shower. She wrapped a towel around her body when done. Then she took a good amount of moisturizer and smoothed it out over her face, neck, hands and legs. She put on her new dress. She dabbed some compact over her face and neck and put a pink lipstick on her lips. Then she combed her hair and let it fall over her shoulders.

She took the scarf that Gloria had gifted her and tied it around her neck, then put on her sandals. She looked at herself in the mirror for some time, adjusting her dress and her hair. Finally, when she was satisfied with her looks, she headed for the Smiths' house.

There were a lot of people in the garden. She looked around for Sophie but couldn't see her. She must be in her room, Maya thought. She tried to make her way to her room but there were a lot of people inside the house too, so she went to the kitchen to find her mom.

Jane was wiping the dishes when Maya entered. She kept staring at her daughter when she saw her.

"You look lovely," she said, squeezing her hands. "Why don't you go out and enjoy."

"But I don't know anyone," Maya kept her voice low, "I would rather stay here."

"Why don't you help me then?" Jane filled a tray with mini muffins for kids and asked Maya to take them out in the garden. Maya carried it out and placed it on a big table beside juice glasses. She looked around and was amazed by how beautiful the house looked with all the decorations. There were flowers everywhere. Kids were running around in the garden with balloons in their hands.

A little later, the ceremony started. Sophie emerged from the house holding her dad's hand. In a big white wedding gown, she looked like a princess from a fairy tale. The twins were walking behind her with flowers in their hands. There was a soft music playing as they walked along the garden. Everyone was looking at the bride, admiring her, some women even started to cry. Jane came and stood beside Maya, holding her hand.

Sophie walked towards the patio where George was standing with another man. The vows were made, rings were exchanged, and then they kissed. Maya tilted her head a bit and smiled at them. Everyone clapped and cheered.

Later, when Sophie and George were by themselves, Maya walked up to them and congratulated them. Sophie hugged her and introduced her to George. They both looked very happy. Other people came forward to congratulate the new bride and groom. Maya took a few steps back and went inside the house. Finding her mom busy in the kitchen, she went away without saying anything to anyone.

Maya took her sandals off when she reached home, then pulled the scarf away. She saw her reflection as she walked past the mirror and stood still for a moment. She liked the way she looked. Then she started to imagine how she would look in a wedding dress. She walked towards the mirror slowly and touched it with her fingertips as if she was touching her beautiful dress. Moving closer, she pressed her lips on the mirror, imagining she was being kissed by her man. The surface of the mirror felt cold against her lips. Does it feel the same way when you kiss someone? She wondered.

Suddenly, she snapped as if breaking from a spell. She smiled and shook her head for acting so stupid. She changed out of her new dress and went into the kitchen to find something to eat. With just a cup of coffee in the morning, she was starving by now.

Jane came home late that night, all exhausted. Seeing lights in Maya's room, she peeked in through the door. Maya was in her bed, reading a book.

"I thought you were asleep by now," she said, and went in to sit beside her.

"I was waiting for you to be home." Maya smiled.

"You disappeared without a word." Jane sounded curious.

"Yeah, I went to find you, but you were busy, so I left. I was getting bored all by myself," Maya replied.

Jane nodded her head slowly. She understood her daughter well and thought she might have felt uncomfortable among the strangers.

"Oh, did I tell you that you looked beautiful in your new dress?" Jane said.

"Yes, mom, you already did." Maya chuckled.

"You know, when everyone was looking at Sophie, I was imagining you as a bride. How lovely you would look in a wedding gown." Jane sounded dreamy.

"I don't want that kind of wedding, mom." Maya was serious suddenly.

"What? But why?" Jane had a perplexed look on her face.

"I don't want a bunch of people staring at me," Maya said.

Jane smiled, but her smile faded away when Maya spoke again.

"I don't have my dad to give me away," Maya said, looking away from her mother.

"Oh honey!" Jane said, holding her hands. She felt a pang in her heart. Maya tilted her head to rest on her mother's shoulder and closed her eyes.

Jane had no words to comfort her. She rested her head on Maya's and rubbed her hand gently with her thumb.

Nine

It had been more than a year since Maya started working at the café and nothing much had changed around. She had become closer with Gloria as a friend. Because of their gossips, Maya had also felt more comfortable chatting, and she would do so with the regular customers too. However, with new customers, she was still shy.

One afternoon, around closing time, two men entered the café: one was in his mid-fifties and the other was young, maybe in his early twenties. Instead of taking seats around the table, they walked towards the counter. Maya turned around to look at them again. This time, the young man caught her eyes and she looked away.

Wendy walked around the counter and hugged them both. She looked happy to see them. Gloria came out of the change room and rushed towards them. Maya was about to enter the change room when Wendy called her.

"Would you mind getting us all some coffee before you go? Thank you, darling."

"Sure," Maya said, and went into the kitchen.

When she came out, all were seated around a table, deep in conversation. She put the cups down on the table and walked away without a word, so as not to disturb them. She was in the change room when Gloria peeked in through the door and said that she could go home as they would be staying a bit longer.

After changing, Maya said good-bye to the boys in the kitchen and waved at Gloria.

"See ya!" Gloria waved back.

Maya smiled at Gloria and Wendy as she walked out, avoiding the looks from the men.

After a few days, Gloria mentioned that it was her birthday on Friday. She was planning to meet her friends in a local pub for the big night, and asked Maya to come along. Maya was hesitant at first.

"Come on, it's my twenty first!" Gloria pleaded. "We'll have fun!"

"I don't know your friends," Maya said.

"So what? You will get to know them when you meet them. And Bob is coming too," Gloria said.

"I haven't been to a pub before," Maya was trying to find an excuse to avoid it.

"So? It will be your first time. You will enjoy it, I promise!" Gloria grinned.

Maya gave in, realizing that Gloria wouldn't give up.

On Friday morning, when Gloria came to the café, Maya wished her happy birthday and gave her a small box. Gloria grinned and opened the box. Inside were a pair of sparkly earrings.

"Wow. Thanks." Gloria hugged her. "I love them," she said.

At five o'clock, they closed the café and quickly cleared the tables.

"See ya at seven!" Gloria shouted as she darted through the doors.

Maya hurried towards home, had a quick shower and changed into a pair of jeans and a top. She thought she would rather put some makeup on, then combed her hair and pinned it to one side. She was ready and about to leave when the yellow scarf caught her eyes. Thinking Gloria might be pleased to see her wearing it, she wrapped it around her neck and made a knot at the side.

She met Jane at the door, who was just returning home from work. Maya had told her earlier that she was going to the pub with Gloria and her friends for her birthday celebration.

"Bye, mom," Maya said, as she passed her.

"Have a good time and don't be late," Jane said, watching her girl as she left.

Maya reached the pub a little before seven, and it was already filled with people. There was music in the background, everyone had a glass of beer in their hands and were busy talking. Maya had no idea what to do. Should she wait outside or go inside? She was not sure. Then she thought, maybe Gloria had arrived already and was inside the pub. Feeling a bit awkward, she walked inside, hoping she would find her in there.

She looked around but couldn't see her. There were wooden stools at the end of the room. Maya went to the corner and sat on a stool to avoid the crowd. Her eyes were fixed at the entrance as she waited for Gloria.

After a few minutes, she spotted Bob. When he saw Maya in the corner waving at him, he walked towards her. They talked for some time, then Bob went to get himself a beer. He asked Maya if she wanted a drink, but she politely declined. He returned with his drink and they talked some more.

At around quarter past seven, Gloria entered with her friends: two girls and one guy whose hand she was holding. She saw Maya and Bob at the corner and went towards them. She made the introductions; the man she was holding hands with was her boyfriend, Mark. She noticed the scarf Maya was wearing and showed her ears. She was wearing the earrings Maya had gifted her that morning. Maya smiled.

"Let's get some drinks," Gloria said.

They went to the bartender and asked for beer for everyone. She gave a glass to Maya who looked skeptical.

"I know it's your first time, darling, but you got to try it sometime," Gloria whispered in her ear. She raised her own glass and winked at her.

Maya lifted the glass to her lips and sipped a little. It isn't that bad, she thought, and sipped some more.

Gloria was smiling at her.

"Happy birthday, Gloria," someone said from behind Maya. Before she could turn around, he walked past her towards Gloria and hugged her.

"Hey, thanks," Gloria said. She looked very happy to see him. "Everyone, this is Daniel, my cousin," she introduced him to everyone.

When she introduced him to Maya, he repeated her name in a soft tone. "Nice to meet you," he said, extending his hand towards her.

Maya took his hand and shook it, swallowing a mouthful of beer she had just sipped. Before she could say anything, he was shaking hands with the others. It took Maya a moment to recognize him: he was the same guy who was at the café a few days ago.

Gloria started to tap her foot, swaying her hips to the music. Then she dragged her boyfriend to the center of the room for a dance. Her friends followed, leaving behind Maya and Daniel.

Daniel extended his hand again towards Maya as if to ask for something. Maya dreaded that he would ask her to dance, but instead he reached for the glass she was holding, which was empty now. Maya sighed in relief.

"Would you like another drink?" he politely asked her.

Maya shook her head. Daniel signaled towards the stools at the counter and walked towards them. Maya followed him. He got himself a glass of beer and sat on one of the stools, Maya sat on the one beside him. Whether it was the beer or the crowd in the room, Maya started to warm up. She loosened her scarf, pulled it off her neck and wrapped it around her wrist.

She sat on the stool with crossed legs and watched the group dance to the music. She checked from the corner of her eye: Daniel was having a chat with the bartender. When he turned to face her, she looked at him and smiled, he smiled back but neither of them said anything.

Gloria rushed towards Maya, giggling and whispered something in her ear. Maya got up and both of them walked towards the ladies' room. As they were leaving, the yellow scarf slipped off Maya's wrist and fell on the floor. Neither of them noticed, but Daniel did. He bent over to pick it up, knowing it was Maya's. He intended to return it, so he kept holding it in his hand. The girls were taking forever though, so he slid it into his pocket and grabbed his beer.

In the ladies' room, Maya felt a bit dizzy. When she told Gloria, she chuckled.

"You just had one glass," she said.

"I should leave now, or my mom will get worried." Maya remembered her mom saying not to be late.

"Are you sure? How are feeling now?" Gloria was concerned.

"All good. I had a good time. You carry on," Maya smiled and hugged her.

She made her way through the crowd towards the main door and started to walk slowly towards her home. The air outside was fresh and she inhaled deeply. She was glad that Gloria had asked her to come. She did enjoy it.

Ten

He had arrived early at the pub, asked for a beer at the counter and seated himself on a stool. He looked around; there were a few people scattered in the room, everyone with a friend or a partner. Sipping his beer, he talked with the bartender, occasionally looking towards the entrance.

"Waiting for someone, mate?" the bartender had asked.

"I'm here for my cousin's twenty-first," he had replied.

As time passed on, more people filled into the room. And then, when she entered, he recognized her instantly. The girl from Wendy's café, he thought.

She looked around the room, searching for someone, then went towards the corner. She was sitting by herself, facing the entrance. Daniel thought he should go talk to her but dismissed the idea as soon as it had come into his mind. She might not even recognize me, he thought.

When Gloria introduced them, she did not say a word to him. She shook his hand, gulped down some beer and blinked her eyes but did not say anything. He found her amusing.

Later when others were dancing, the two of them were sitting at the counter. He wanted to talk to her but felt that she was trying to avoid any talks, so he didn't push further.

After picking up her scarf, he was waiting so he could give it to her and start from there, but she did not return. Instead, Gloria announced later that she had left, and he felt a bit disappointed.

When she was in bed, Maya kept thinking about the evening. Her first experience wasn't that bad. She thought about Daniel too, she had sensed that he wanted to talk to her, but she was not comfortable. One thing she liked about him was that he had not tried to drag her into any conversation. He might have sensed her hesitance. He had repeated her name when Gloria had introduced them. Did he find her name interesting too, just like Gloria did the first time they had met? she thought.

Her mom had once mentioned to her about how she came across the name. While she was working for a wealthy family before the Smiths, she had met their friends from abroad who were there on a holiday. One of the ladies' names was Maya. She was beautiful and gentle and was very polite to Jane. Jane had liked her instantly. Years later when she had a baby girl, she couldn't think of any other name for her.

When Maya met Gloria at the café on the next working day, she asked her how she felt later that evening after leaving the pub. Maya said that she had been fine and had a good time that evening.

"See, I told you that you would enjoy it." Gloria was grinning. She said that they had stayed for another couple of hours.

"Everyone?" Maya asked.

"Yeah, except Daniel. He left about half an hour later you did. He had to sleep early as he was leaving the next day," Gloria said.

"Leaving?" Maya was curious.

"Oh, silly me. I didn't mention that he lives in Sydney, did I? He lives there with his uncle and was here for a short trip." Gloria went on to explain, "His uncle has a restaurant in Sydney and is planning to move his business here to Perth. So, he came here to have a look around and get some idea from Aunt Wendy. Daniel had a short break, so he came along too. He goes to college, you know."

"You said you were cousins," Maya seemed to be more interested.

"Yep," Gloria said, "My mom, Aunt Wendy, and his mom are sisters."

"Oh!" Maya nodded her head and said nothing more.

On that night in the pub, Daniel had been sitting by himself at the counter with his glass in his hand. Gloria and her friends were drunk. He started to get a bit bored. When Gloria came to the counter for some more beer, he told her that he had to leave early. He left after saying good-bye to everyone. Walking through the street, he realized that for a Friday night, it was much quieter here than in Sydney.

He went to the hotel where he was staying with his uncle. They had booked a room with two single beds. He opened the door with his keys and entered quietly. He checked in on his uncle, David, who was snoring in his bed. Daniel changed his clothes and slid under the blanket in his bed. He hadn't bothered to turn the lights on so as not to disturb his uncle.

A few days earlier, David had asked him if he would like to go on a trip with him. Since Daniel was on a break, he had agreed. He liked spending time with his uncle, and after getting into college, he had been quite busy. David had a small restaurant in the town. Daniel worked there during study breaks and helped David to keep the accounts.

Daniel had been living with David since he was a kid. He hardly remembered his own parents. David never mentioned them, but his grandparents had told him about his parents.

His grandparents had migrated to Australia from England. After a year's struggle, they had established themselves as successful businessmen. In a couple of years, they had their first son, David. A year after that, they had their second son, Daniel's father. They both grew to be handsome gentlemen.

David found his love when he was twenty-four. They declared that they were deeply in love and got married within a year. He loved her so much that when she passed away unexpectedly after a few years, he decided to stay single forever.

Daniel's mother was very young when she had met his father. She was seventeen and he was twenty-three. After a few dates, they announced that they were in love and got married the next year. They had Daniel within a year.

Daniel's mother was vibrant. She loved to party, and would get drunk occasionally. Having a baby had changed her life and she was not able to cope well with it. She used to get stressed and started to drink even more. When her husband tried to talk to her about it, they would end up in a fight. Their love life was going downhill as Daniel was growing up. When he turned two, his mother left the house one day, leaving behind a note that said she wanted a divorce. Before the divorce was finalized, she was already seeing another man.

Daniel's father was heartbroken when she left. He told his parents that he couldn't live there anymore and wanted to go to England to start something new. He wanted to take Daniel with him, but his parents refused. They knew that he was in no state to raise a child.

That was when Uncle David had decided to be his guardian. After losing his wife, David had been miserable, and he thought he had no purpose in his life. When Daniel came along, he had a reason to live. He started to smile again, and his heart was filled with love once more. Little Daniel brought happiness into his life.

David had raised him well, and Daniel had grown into a kind, well behaved gentleman. He was good looking too, attracting female attention all the time. When he worked in the restaurant, lady customers would stare at him. Girls in his college would find a reason to talk to him. Some wanted to be his friend, and some even asked him out, but he was a bit shy with girls. Being raised by his uncle, Daniel had never got a chance to be close with any woman. David had never dated anyone while Daniel was growing up.

Daniel did go out with a couple of girls after they insisted. They were way too excited for a coffee date and talked a lot. He was never interested in any of them.

He rather preferred spending time with his uncle. When they both had free time, they would surf and go for a swim in the sea. Once a week, they would go fishing. David must have noticed his behavior regarding girls, so he talked about it once while they were fishing.

"You cannot fish at home, Daniel. You have to come out to the sea to catch them," David said, as he prepared his fishing line.

"Of course," Daniel laughed lightly.

"You got to open up and meet more girls," David went on, without looking at him.

"To catch a fish?" Daniel stared at his uncle, not understanding the connection between a fish and a girl.

"No, no," David laughed, "To catch the one girl who is meant for you." He looked at Daniel in his eyes, but he still looked confused. "How are you going to find your love if you keep avoiding every girl?" he said.

Daniel finally got what his uncle was trying to say to him. He looked away and worked on his fishing line. "If I met her, how would I know that she is the one?" he asked in a low voice.

"You will know," David said, "You won't be able to get her off your mind."

"Were you not able to get your true love off your mind when you met her?" The words came out of his mouth before he could stop himself.

"I still can't." David was staring at the sea. "She is still on my mind all the time."

Eleven

It had been some time since that talk. After listening to his uncle, Daniel had tried. He had opened up, talked with girls when he met them, and went on dates with a few of them, but was never interested in any of them. No one had left an impression on his mind the next day.

After their short trip to Perth, both were back to their normal routines. David was busy in his restaurant and Daniel kept himself busy between college and the restaurant. A couple of months had passed, and Christmas holidays were ahead. One evening, David told him that they were closing early and asked him to get dressed.

"We are going for a drink," he said.

They used to occasionally go to a bar on weekends for a few drinks. But, it was a weekday and Daniel wondered why his uncle was in a mood for a drink.

Daniel was ready to go and was waiting for David, who came out a little later, all dressed up. David celebrated 'the day he had met his love' every year. He called it their 'love anniversary'.

At the bar, they sat in front of the counter with drinks in their hands. Staring at his drink, David seemed to be lost in his thoughts. Daniel thought it was better not to disturb him, so he didn't say anything. It amazed him how his uncle was still in love with his long-gone wife.

"Love is a wonderful thing." David finally spoke up, "It gives you the happiness that you were unaware of. I never knew how happy I could be until I met her. She made me complete."

"Don't you feel sad that she is gone?" Daniel asked softly. He felt sad that his uncle was alone.

"I do." David sighed. "It was not fair that she died so early. I miss her every day. But I am also happy that we met, fell in love and spend some wonderful time together." He looked distant for a moment, as if living those memories again.

"I hope you will find your love too, my boy," David said. "And when you do, love her with all your heart."

Daniel was quiet. He didn't know what to say. They asked for more drinks and continued to chat. After about an hour, they left for home. Saying their goodnights, they went to their rooms.

Daniel kept thinking about what his uncle had said at the bar. Before changing his clothes, he slipped his hand in his pants' pocket and pulled out some coins. He put the coins on a table and went for another pocket. His fingers touched something soft. Not remembering what he had in his pocket, he pulled it out. It was a yellow silk scarf. Strangely enough, he had not worn these pants since the night of Gloria's birthday in Perth.

"Maya!" her name slipped out of his mouth. After he had picked up the scarf, he hadn't gotten the chance to return it and had put it in his pocket. The next day, he had left for Sydney and had totally forgotten about it.

Now as he held it in his hand, he thought about Maya. He remembered how she had looked away when he had looked at her in the café. Usually, girls stared at him and were eager to talk to him, but Maya was just the opposite. She had avoided any talks with him at the pub and had left without a good-bye.

He put the scarf on the bed and went to get changed. When he returned to his bed, he lifted the scarf again and laid down holding it in his hand. He kept thinking about her until he fell asleep.

When he woke up the next morning, the scarf was on his pillow. He grabbed it and pulled it towards his nose, trying to smell it. The image of Maya entering the pub flashed before his eyes, how he noticed the yellow scarf around her neck. He smiled and got off his bed, then walked towards his closet where he hung the scarf next to his clothes.

Every time he changed his clothes, he would see it and think about Maya. He started to wonder what she was like, what did she prefer to do? The more he thought about her, the more he was interested in knowing her. He wanted to meet her and talk to her, but that seemed impossible right away.

David had noticed the change in his behavior. He looked dreamy most of the time as if thinking about something or someone.

"Everything okay with you, my boy?" David asked him once, when he caught him staring out of the window while holding a book in his hand.

"Yeah," Daniel said, pretending to focus on his book.

David gave him a skeptical look and walked away.

"What is wrong with me?" Daniel thought, "She might not even remember that I exist and here I am thinking about her." He sighed, trying not to think about her anymore, but in vain.

It was a week before Christmas when he finally decided that he had to go see her. "I want to go to Perth for a few days," he announced at the dinner table one evening.

David stopped his fork midway to his mouth and stared at him. "What is cooking in your head?" he asked with a raised eyebrow.

"Fish," Daniel answered, without thinking.

"What?" David almost dropped his fork.

"Uh, nothing," Daniel mumbled, "I have to see someone."

David smiled. He knew better than to ask anything further. Later, he gave Daniel a sheet of paper and said that it had addresses of some places he was considering for opening a restaurant. He asked him if he could have a look around while he was there.

Daniel packed a few clothes for his short trip. The last thing he put in his travel bag was the yellow scarf. He was very excited and anxious at the same time for his trip. What was he doing? Should he even go there? He wondered, but he knew that he had to see her once.

He checked into the same hotel when he reached Perth. At first, he thought he would go to the café the next day, but he couldn't wait anymore. He took a quick shower and changed into casual jeans and a t-shirt. The hotel he stayed at was close to the café, so he walked towards it.

He met Aunt Wendy at the counter. She was surprised but pleased to see him and asked him what brought him there. He said that David had sent him to inspect a few places that he was considering for his restaurant.

They were interrupted by a customer who had come to make their payment. "Why don't you have something. You must be hungry." Wendy signaled him towards the table.

Daniel nodded and went for a table at the far end, hoping Maya would come to take his order. He looked around but couldn't see her.

Gloria saw him and almost ran towards him. "Daniel!" she cried, "What are you doing here?"

He stood up and kissed her on her cheeks and repeated the same story he had told Wendy.

Gloria was excited to see him and wouldn't stop talking. Daniel was nodding his head, trying to look interested, but his eyes were wandering around the café. He started to wonder if Maya had even come to the café that day or if she still worked there. He hadn't thought about it before he left, and now sitting here, a sense of fear crept over him.

But his fear washed away as soon as he saw her coming out of the kitchen with a handful. He inhaled deeply, watching her as she placed the food on the other customer's table. He found her beautiful, even in her apron. He was hoping that she would notice him and come to say hello.

Maya moved onto the next table to take an order. When she was done, she looked around as if to check on any new customers. For a moment, Daniel thought that she looked at him and was hopeful, but she went back into the kitchen without noticing him.

He swallowed hard as his mouth went dry. Gloria was still talking but he wasn't listening. He couldn't focus anymore; he had to get out of there. He told Gloria that he had to be somewhere and would see her the next day. Before she could say anything, he was up and striding out of the café.

Earlier in the excitement, he hadn't noticed the heat, but now as he returned to his hotel, he realized that it was very hot here. In his room, he kept thinking about what he had done. They had not even talked when they met last time and he had come all the way to see her. What was he thinking? He thought he had made a fool of himself. She had looked in his direction but there was no sign of recognition on her face. She sure wasn't interested in him. It was just him who was acting like an idiot. He laid on his bed but couldn't sleep, unaware that Maya was wide awake in her bed too.

Laying on her bed, she was staring at the ceiling, thinking about her day. It had been a few months, she had almost forgotten about him and there he was today, as if to remind her about him. She had seen him chatting with Gloria, so she went into the kitchen with her order. When she came out, he was gone.

She was a bit disappointed. She was sure it was him. She couldn't have mistaken his handsome features. She had expected to talk with him, but he had disappeared without a word. Maybe he was not interested in talking with her. And why would he be, she thought, after the way she had avoided talking with him the last time they had met.

She would have talked with him today, she wanted to, but he was gone before she had a chance.

Twelve

The next day while working, Maya found herself thinking about Daniel most of the time. She tried to stop herself from doing so, reminding herself that he did not even live in the same city and there was no chance to meet him again. She could have asked Gloria about him but then thought it was better not to.

Daniel woke up late that morning. Since his mission was over, he didn't feel like getting out of bed, but he had to visit a few places for his uncle. He dragged himself out of the bed and went to the bathroom, brushed his teeth and washed his face but didn't bother to shave. After changing his clothes, he went out, searching for a place to eat. He hadn't had anything since yesterday and was starving by now. He could have gone to Wendy's café but didn't feel like it. After a heavy breakfast, he went searching for the addresses one by one, making a few notes about the places and their surroundings.

By the end of the day, Daniel was very hot and tired. He knew there was a river near the city. Since he had nothing to do, he thought of going there to shake off the heat. Asking for the direction with the locals, he walked towards the river. He found a bench and sat on it, too tired to walk along the bank. The cool air helped him relax. It was quiet and peaceful. He sat there for a long time staring at the water as it slowly flowed.

Maya had headed for home after closing the café but it was very hot outside. At the junction, she turned towards the Swan River instead. When she reached there, she sat on the grass with her legs stretched out in front of her. As usual, she sat there and observed the water, the birds and the people. After taking her time, she got up and strolled along the bank.

She saw him a little ahead of her, sitting on a bench and staring at the river. He looked a bit different than yesterday; he looked tired. For a moment, she debated in her mind whether she should talk to him or not. Then she took a deep breath and walked towards him. Deep in his thoughts, he didn't notice her approaching him.

"Daniel," she said softly.

He looked towards her and kept staring at her, lost for words.

"Hi!" she said with a smile.

"Umm. Hi," he said. He stood up and extended his hand towards her. He couldn't believe his eyes; he thought he was dreaming.

"How are you?" Maya asked, as she shook his hand.

"I am good. How are you?" he asked, he was still finding it hard to believe.

"Good, good," she said, and sat down on the bench.

Daniel sat down slowly. He wanted to look at her face but looked ahead instead. Is this really happening? he was thinking.

"What brings you here? Gloria mentioned that you live in Sydney," Maya asked casually.

"My uncle wanted me to visit some sites for him," Daniel replied. "He is considering opening a restaurant here."

Maya nodded. Both were quiet for some time.

"It's nice and cool here," Daniel said.

"Yes, I come here often," Maya said.

I'm glad you do, Daniel thought. They were quiet again.

"I should go now. My mom gets worried if I am too late." Maya stood up.

Daniel got on his feet too but didn't want her to leave yet.

"It was good to see you," Maya said softly, looking into his eyes.

"Nice meeting you too," Daniel said with a nod.

Maya smiled, turned around and started to walk away slowly.

Daniel was struggling for words to stop her. He met her with a stroke of luck and couldn't let her go just like that.

"Maya!" He called her with a shaky voice. Maya turned around swiftly. He walked towards her. "Can I see you again?" he asked.

"Umm…" Maya wasn't sure how to reply to that.

"I have something that belongs to you and I want to return it," Daniel said in one breath.

"What is it?" Maya looked confused.
"Lunch tomorrow?" Daniel was almost begging.
"Okay." Maya smiled.
Daniel let go of the breath that he had been holding.
"I'll wait outside your café." He sounded excited.
"Okay, see you then." Maya waved and turned around.
"See ya," Daniel said, as he waved at her.
Maya turned her head to look at him and smiled.

He stood there, looking at her as she walked away. He stood there for as long as he could see her before she disappeared around the corner. He had given up all hopes of seeing her or meeting her again, and all of a sudden, there she was, standing next to him, calling his name. She had even agreed to meet him again, though he practically begged her. He was very happy and very excited for their lunch date the next day.

Maya had surprised herself by going up to him and talking to him. More than that, by agreeing to meet him the next day. She wondered what he had that belonged to her; she couldn't think of what it would be.

The next morning, Maya was excited and nervous at the same time. She informed Wendy first thing in the morning that she would leave early for lunch that day. It was busy during lunch time as usual and though she tried her best, she was late. She went to the change room to take her apron off, adjusted her skirt and blouse, and brushed her hair with her fingers. She applied lipstick that she had carried in her purse, then hurried towards the main door.

She looked around and saw him standing at the far end of the block, waving at her. Daniel smiled as she got closer and so did she.

"Did I keep you waiting for long? The café is busy during lunch time," Maya explained for being late.

"No worries! I've been here for a few minutes only," Daniel said. Looking at him, Maya knew that he had been out in the heat for more than just a few minutes.

In the excitement, Daniel was out of bed early. He had taken a shower, shaved and then changed into jeans and a shirt. After a cup of coffee, he was out of the hotel. Though it was still too early for lunch, he couldn't wait in the hotel, so he thought he would roam around the city. When it was about time, he went and waited for Maya, a bit further from the café.

It was getting hot, but he stood there, his eyes fixed at the café's entrance. It had been more than an hour when Maya came out of the café. He waved his hand as she was searching for him. Though she had been working from the morning, she looked fresh and beautiful.

Maya noticed that he had shaved; she even caught a hint of cologne as they walked together. They strolled along a few blocks and onto another street, then entered one of the food outlets. They both were quiet for some time, just smiling at one another.

"How's your uncle?" Maya asked.

"He is doing good," Daniel replied.

"How is the weather in Sydney?" she asked.

"It's much cooler than here," he said, "But the weather here is perfect for the beach, don't you think so?"

"Yeah." Maya smiled and looked out of the window. It had been ages since she had been to the beach.

Daniel noticed that she wasn't very excited about the beach. Their food arrived: an egg and bacon sandwich for

Daniel and salad for Maya. They started to eat, talking about the cities they lived in, their families and work. When he asked about her family, she told him that it was just her and her mom. She even told him that her father had left when she was a kid. Daniel told her about his parents and how his uncle had raised him.

Maya remembered what he had said the other day.

"So, what is it you have that belongs me? I couldn't think of anything." She thought that he had made up the story to see her.

"Oh yes!" he said. He had almost forgotten about it. He wiped his hands and went for his pants' pocket. When he brought his hand up on the table, there was the yellow scarf in it.

Maya almost gasped; she couldn't believe her eyes.

"How did you get it? I noticed it was missing and couldn't find it anywhere," she said as she held the scarf in her hand and looked at him with questionable eyes.

Daniel was enjoying this moment and the look in her eyes.

"You had dropped it in the pub. I picked it up and waited for you to return so that I could give it to you, but you had left without a good-bye," he explained.

Maya relaxed a bit when the mystery was solved. "Thank you," she said, "And sorry for leaving without a word that night. I was not feeling well to stay any longer." She knew she did not need to explain it now, but she wanted to.

"Don't bother," Daniel waved his hand. "I am glad we met again," he added.

"Me too," she said softly.

Maya noticed the clock on the wall and realized she was getting late. "I would love to stay but I should get back to work now," she said.

Daniel stood up and went to pay for their food.

"Have you done what you were here for?" Maya asked him on their way back to the café.

"Yes, I have," Daniel replied. He was here to see her, but he knew she was asking about visiting the sites for his Uncle David.

"Thanks for coming for lunch today," he said, looking ahead.

"I had to," Maya replied.

"I'll see you again," he said casually, but had no idea when or where. He just wanted to see her again.

"When are you leaving?" Maya asked.

"Soon," he replied.

"I had a good time." She smiled.

"Me too," he said.

"Bye!" Maya waved her hand and marched towards the café.

Daniel looked on as she entered through the doors. He was glad that he had met her and now that she was gone, he wanted to see her again.

It was around closing time. Maya was in the kitchen, waiting for the food that her customer had ordered. It was hot in here, she wondered how the boys cooked all day in such heat. When the food was ready, she carried the tray out.

For a moment, she thought she saw Daniel standing at the counter. Then she thought she must be dreaming; she had been thinking about him all day and now she was seeing him too. She shook her head and blinked her eyes, but when she opened them, he was still there. She wasn't dreaming, he was there, chatting with Gloria and Wendy.

Maya walked with extra care so as not to trip while carrying her food. She went on to place the food on the table of her awaiting customer.

"Maya!" She heard Gloria calling her.

She turned around and went towards them.

"You remember Daniel? You met him at the pub," Gloria said.

"Yes. How are you?" Maya smiled at Daniel.

"Good. How are you?" Daniel extended his hand towards her.

"Good." Maya shook his hand.

"We are going to beach tomorrow. Why don't you join us?" Gloria said to Maya.

It was the weekend and Maya had no other plans. It looked like the weather was going to be perfect too. It had been a long time since Maya had been to the beach. She knew that it was Daniel's idea; she could tell by the look on his face. She agreed and it was decided that Gloria would pick her up the next morning.

Thirteen

Maya chose blue shorts and a white shirt to wear for the day. She let her hair fall free and pulled a hair band over her wrist just in case she had to tie her hair. She was putting on her thongs when she heard a horn honking outside. Kissing her mom on her cheeks, she hurried towards the door.

Gloria was in the front seat with Mark at the wheel. Maya said hello to both. She was concerned for not seeing Daniel but didn't say anything. Gloria then said that they would go to the hotel where Daniel was staying to pick him up.

Within a few minutes they pulled over in front of a hotel and Daniel jogged towards them. He was waiting at the entrance; his excitement was obvious. He climbed in the back seat, and as he sat beside Maya, he grinned at her.

Gloria kept talking throughout their drive while others were listening. When they reached the beach, Mark pulled over behind some sand dunes. Gloria jumped out of the car and went behind to open the trunk. She pulled out a blanket and a couple of towels. There was an esky which Daniel offered to carry, and they all walked towards the sea.

Gloria spread the blanket on the sand a few feet away from the water and dropped the towels on it. She took her top and shorts off and dropped them too.

"Come on," she said to Mark, and ran towards the sea. Mark took his shirt off and followed her into the water.

Maya sat on the blanket, giggling as she watched Gloria splashing in the waves. Daniel put the esky down beside him and sat next to Maya.

"This is so good," Maya said, as she breathed in deeply, closing her eyes.

"Been some time?" Daniel asked.

"Years," she replied, with her eyes still closed.

Daniel looked at her with surprise but didn't say anything.

"You go to the beach often?" she asked him.

"Yeah," he said, "I surf every week, go fishing with my Uncle David, sometimes watch the sun as it sets. You should come to the beach in the evening, it's beautiful."

Maya looked at him and smiled.

"You won't join them?" she asked, looking towards Gloria and Mark who were having a great time splashing one another.

"And you?" he asked her.

"I'll stay here," she replied.

Daniel didn't force her to come. Instead, he got up, took his shirt off, and jogged ahead. He dived into the coming waves and swam further into the sea. Maya could tell that he was a strong swimmer. She watched him as he made powerful strokes. He had a body of an athlete, and she enjoyed watching him in the water.

After a while, she got up and strolled barefoot along the beach. She continued walking further, bending down on her knees occasionally to pick up some shells. There were kids making sandcastles, and some parents helping their kids in the water. Some boys were playing ball on the sand. There were couples laying side by side on their towel, soaking in the sun, and some were walking along the beach holding hands.

It was the weekend and the weather was hot. There was a crowd; lots of people lying on the sand and many in the water. Some were playing with the waves in the shallows while others were swimming further into the sea. She had no idea how far she had gone; her one hand was full of shells.

She turned around to return, and a gush of wind blew her hair over her face. Holding her hair away from her face with one hand and carrying shells in the other, she strode towards their spot. She found Daniel and Gloria sitting on the blanket, munching on sandwiches.

"Help yourself," Gloria said, pointing towards the esky.

Maya put her shells down and tied her hair.

"You've got a collection there," Daniel said, looking at her shells.

Maya smiled, then grabbed a sandwich and sat beside Gloria, folding her legs at the knee to one side.

"You enjoying the beach?" Gloria asked Maya.

"Yeah," she replied with a nod.

"Good," she said, gulped down some water and went to join Mark again.

"Could you pass me some water please?" Daniel requested to Maya.

"Sure," she said, and picked a bottle of water from the esky. She extended it towards him, who stretched his hand to reach it. His fingers brushed hers for a second. She felt a tingle but pretended not to notice.

"Wanna go swim?" Daniel asked her when they had finished eating.

"I can't," Maya said in a hesitant voice. "Never tried," she added.

"You can play in the waves," he suggested.

"I'm not sure," she tried to protest.

"Come on." He got on his feet, "You can't go home dry after coming to a beach."

Maya didn't make any move.

"You can hold my hand," he said, offering his hand. "Come on."

Maya gave in, and holding his hand, pulled herself up.

They jogged together holding hands. The water felt cool against her feet. Daniel pulled her further into the sea. As the waves came and went, she could feel the sand beneath her feet giving way and she held onto Daniel's hand more tightly.

They kept moving further, and the water was up to her waist now. The waves hit her stomach, so she turned around to face the other way. The waves were hitting hard on her back and she was having a hard time balancing herself.

"It hurts where the waves break, we should go in further," Daniel said.

As they moved on, water was up to her chest now. Maya was scared; she had never been in such deep water.

"Don't let me go," she almost shouted.

"I won't. I promise," Daniel said, in a serious tone.

A big wave was approaching them, Maya panicked.

"Hold tight and jump when I say," Daniel said.

"What?" Maya shouted.

The wave was just inches away. Maya thought she was going to drown with it.

"Now. Jump!" She heard Daniel shout and she jumped.

She was swept by the wave gently, it felt like she was riding it. When her feet touched the sand again, she smiled and then giggled. Her eyes were sparkling when she looked at Daniel.

"Again!" she shouted excitedly.

Daniel grinned and they both waited for another go and then another.

When Maya was satisfied, they went for the shore. She felt the chill when the cool breeze blew through her wet swimsuit. Her wet hair fell over her shoulders, a few strands over her face, water dripping from them. Daniel found her even more beautiful, unable to take his eyes off her. Realizing they were still holding hands, Maya pulled hers away and went to sit on the blanket. Daniel followed her.

"That was amazing," she said. Daniel sat beside her. "Thank you so much," she added, looking at him.

"It was my pleasure." He smiled.

They sat there for some time, watching others in the water.

"You want to take a walk? The wind will dry you faster," Daniel said to her.

"Okay," she said, and got up.

They strolled along the beach side by side, talking and laughing like good old friends. They had lost track of time and how far they had walked together. It was the afternoon, but the sun was still bright, and the sky was clear blue. Daniel stooped down to pick up a shell and handed it over to Maya. It was a white shell with a tint of pink and was much bigger than those Maya had collected. She beamed.

"We should get back before Gloria starts searching for us," Maya said.

They both turned around, though Daniel would have loved to spend the evening with her on the beach.

Gloria was lying on the blanket, all heated up.

"Where were you folks?" she asked, opening one eye.

"Went for a walk," Daniel replied.

Before she could say anything further, he went for one last swim.

Gloria stared at Maya who had come to sit beside her.

"What?" Maya asked her when she kept staring at her.

"Is there anything I should know?" Gloria asked, raising her eyebrow.

"Nope," Maya answered sternly.

"I could see you were enjoying yourself with him in the water and now you went for a walk," she said.

"Aren't we here to enjoy the day?" Maya shrugged. "He is just giving me company since you are busy with Mark," she teased her.

"Okay, okay," Gloria went back to sunbathing. Maya was relieved that her questions had stopped.

The boys came out of the water and relaxed for some time. Then they called it for the day and packed up their belongings into the car. They drove to Maya's house first to drop her off. She mouthed 'thank you' to Daniel as she got out of the car and waved at everyone with a big smile.

Fourteen

As she laid in bed that night, Maya thought about the day while she held the shell Daniel had picked for her, rubbing her thumb gently over it. She kept smiling as she relived the moments of the day. The way she felt when she jumped with the waves, holding his hand, it was the best feeling ever. She hadn't felt anything like that in her life before.

Daniel was thinking about the day too while he lay wide awake in his bed. All he could think about was Maya: the way she looked while playing in the waves, the way she looked with wet hair over her face, the way she shrugged a bit when his fingers touched hers. She was thrilled to be in the water. He had never seen her so happy before and he wanted her to be happy for ever.

It was Sunday the next day. Daniel stayed at the hotel all day as it was too hot to go out. He had to return to Sydney soon, but he couldn't leave without seeing Maya one more time. He could have gone to the café, but it was closed on Sundays. He waited impatiently for the next day. Early the next morning, he headed to the café for breakfast.

Wendy greeted him at the door. "Morning, Daniel. You are in early today," she said in a cheerful voice.

"Morning," he said, with a sweet smile. "I need some coffee."

"Why don't you grab a seat?" Wendy said.

Daniel sat down, hoping that Maya would come to his table. Wendy went to the change room and poked her head through the door.

"Can you get some coffee for Daniel?" she asked Maya who was adjusting her apron.

Maya looked up and stared at Wendy. She wasn't sure if she had heard her right, but before she could question it, Wendy was gone. Maya tugged at her blouse, and made sure her hair was in place, then walked out slowly. She saw him seated at the table, reading a newspaper. Her heart skipped a bit at the sight of him.

"What a pleasant surprise," she wanted to say, but went for a "good morning" instead.

"Good morning," Daniel greeted her, "Can I have a cup of coffee please?"

"How would you like it?" Maya asked.

"Black, no sugar," he replied.

"Sure," she said as she turned around and went towards the kitchen.

She was out with a cup of coffee in no time. He was the only customer in the café since it was early for the regular customers. She placed the coffee in front of him.

"Would you like to have something with your coffee?" she asked.

"What do you suggest?" Daniel asked, sipping his coffee.

"Banana bread," she replied, after a pause.

"I'll have it," he said, with a smile.

When Maya returned with a banana bread, he was scribbling on the newspaper with a pen.

"Enjoy!" she said, with a smile as she placed it on his table.

Just then, two men walked in through the door and took their seats. Maya went to serve them, took their orders and went to the kitchen. She would have loved to share the table with Daniel and enjoy the coffee with him, but she was working.

She noticed that Daniel had finished his coffee and was about to leave. She hurried towards the men and placed their order on the table, then went to Daniel's table to clear it. She wanted to talk to him, at least say something, but she couldn't find the right words. She just smiled while collecting the cup and plate.

"Please read the paper," he said, as he handed the newspaper to her and then walked towards Wendy.

Not knowing what he meant by that, Maya carried the dishes to the kitchen. She stood by the sink, unfolded the newspaper and then read the headlines. She flipped through the pages scanning, until she came across a handwritten note on the top of a page.

It read "Meet me at the riverside after work."

She smiled, reading it again.

"What's so funny in the paper, mate?" Bob asked from the other side.

"Uhm! Nothing," Maya mumbled, and marched out of the door. She checked the counter, but he was gone by then.

Maya was busy throughout the day. After closing the café, she went to the change room, and took her time adjusting her skirt and blouse. She removed the band from her ponytail to let her hair fall free. She was anxious to see him.

The sun was still bright, and it was hot outside as Maya increased her pace towards Swan River. She went straight to the bench where she had seen him the other day. He was sitting on the same bench, waiting for her with flowers in his hand. He stood up as she approached.

"For you," he said, holding out the flowers with a smile.

"Thank you," Maya said, taking them. Though he was smiling, she could sense that something was bothering him. "Are you okay?" She was concerned.

"Umm, yeah," he said, inhaling deeply, then added, "I am leaving tomorrow, wanted to see you before I left."

"Oh!" Maya said slowly.

They both sat on the bench, looking ahead, and were quiet for a long time. She had the most wonderful time these past few days with him, but he would be gone the next day. And the worst part was that she had no idea when he would be back again.

"Can't you stay any longer?" she asked.

"I have to be with Uncle David for Christmas," he explained.

Maya nodded her head, "I'll miss you," Maya reached for his hand.

He was surprised by her gesture. "I'll miss you more," he said, holding her hand between his hands.

The sun was preparing to set, and it was getting cooler. Maya would never have been late for home if it was some other time, but today she wanted to stay a bit longer. She wanted to ask him when he would be back again, but she didn't.

"It's getting late, you should go home now," Daniel said, clearing his throat.

"Yeah," Maya whispered.

Daniel stood first and pulled her up, holding her hand. She knew he was looking at her, but she couldn't meet his gaze.

He followed her as she started to walk away. After taking a few steps, she stopped. She turned around and lifted her head to say something, but before she could say anything, she felt a cool sensation on her lips. It took her sometime to realize that Daniel had kissed her. Her throat went dry and she pulled away quickly.

"Flowers," she could hardly utter the word, as she pointed towards the flowers on the bench. She walked past him, towards them with shaky legs. She had turned around for the flowers that Daniel had given her earlier. She had left them on the bench.

Daniel closed his eyes shut for a moment. He had misunderstood, but he wasn't sorry.

Maya walked ahead, holding the flowers in her hand. Her head felt dizzy and her throat was still dry. She could finish a bottle of water in a gulp right now.

"I'll walk you home," Daniel said from behind, to which Maya didn't respond.

They walked side by side in silence, both thinking in their head about what had happened earlier. Daniel couldn't get a hint about how she was feeling. He had assumed that she liked him too, but what if he was wrong?

"Here we are," Maya looked at him for the first time when they reached her home. He was quiet. "I'll see you again when you visit next time," Maya said.

"Yeah." Daniel's voice was heavy.

"Bye," she said under her breath and went inside.

Daniel stood there for some time, staring at the closed door, then returned to his hotel.

Fifteen

Jane was preparing dinner when Maya walked in. She went to the kitchen, placed the flowers on the table, then sat down on a chair. Jane looked at the flowers and then at her daughter, who looked distant and disturbed.

"Are you okay, darling?" she asked.

"Yeah. I need a shower." Maya went to the bathroom before Jane could question her further.

She couldn't sleep that night. It was her first kiss. She remembered how she used to imagine kissing someone. She tossed and turned in her bed unable to sleep, recalling her every meeting with Daniel.

A knock on the door woke her up in the morning, and she could hear her mother walk in.

"Are you not feeling well?" Jane asked, placing her palm on Maya's forehead.

"I am fine mom, why do you ask?" Her eyes were still shut, and she didn't feel like getting up.

"You are sleeping in late," Jane said.

"What time is it?" Maya peeked through one eye.

"It's nine already," Jane replied.

"What?" Maya sat up straight in a jerk. "I'm late for work," she said.

"You can stay at home if you are not feeling good enough. I will go and fill in for you." Jane was worried that she might be sick.

"No mom, I'm fine. Couldn't sleep last night, that's all." Maya dashed towards the bathroom.

"Have some breakfast, it's ready," Jane said, when Maya came out of the bathroom. "You are late anyway."

Maya thought she was right and sat down on a chair.

Jane placed a cup of coffee, toast and egg in front of her. Maya started to eat in a hurry.

"So, who are the flowers from?" Jane asked finally.

Maya almost choked on her food but continued to eat. Jane was waiting for the reply.

"Daniel!" Maya said without looking at her.

"Who's Daniel?" Jane asked with surprise.

"Gloria's cousin," Maya replied.

Now Jane was more confused than surprised. "Why would Gloria's cousin give you flowers?" she asked.

"Mom, can we talk later? I'm very late." Maya finished her coffee in a gulp and went to her room. After a quick change, she was out of the house. She took a deep breath once she was out. She had not thought that she had to explain things to her mom. What would she say to her? There is this guy who likes her and whom she likes too and now he is gone to another city and she doesn't know when he will be back, if he ever will? She felt helpless.

At the café, she made an excuse of not feeling well. Gloria kept asking her if she was okay.

"You take rest if you need to. I can handle these people." She winked at her.

"Thanks, but I'm okay," Maya smiled back.

She wondered if she should tell her about the other day. How would she react? She would ask hundreds of questions and she was in no mood to answer them, so she kept quiet.

Maya thought about her mother on the way home. Jane would raise the question again and she couldn't avoid her. She had to tell her everything.

As expected, Jane asked her again about Daniel after dinner. Maya told her how she had met him and about all the other meetings after that. Jane listened intently, and her eyes widened when Maya told her about the kiss.

"Did you meet him today? Did you talk about it?" Jane asked her.

"No," Maya looked down, "He has left for Sydney."

"What?" Jane looked confused.

"He lives in Sydney, mom." While telling her mom about their meetings, she had not mentioned that he lived in another city.

"What were you thinking, Maya?" Jane's voice was stern. "Why did you let him get close to you when you knew he did not even live here?"

"I don't know, mom." Maya closed her eyes. "He is a nice man," she said under her breath.

"What's the point when you can't be together?" Jane's question hit Maya like lightning. She hadn't thought about it, but her mom was right. They couldn't be together if they lived apart.

"He is gone, and you let it go too. Don't get carried away. Get a hold of yourself and move on." It sounded more like an order than advice. With that, Jane went to her room.

Sleep was out of question, so Maya went to the back of the house and sat on the steps. She gazed into the sky, staring at the stars like she used to do when she was a kid. Nothing much had changed. She had imaginations growing up and now she had memories, rest was the same.

Daniel was out in his backyard, sitting on a chair, staring at the sky. After he had arrived, he went to meet David in his restaurant. Though it was busy, Daniel did not offer to stay. He told David that he was a bit tired and wanted to rest at home. It was an excuse to be alone.

He kept staring at the sky, thinking about the days he had spent with Maya. Those few days were the most wonderful in his life. He had experienced the feelings that he had not known before. He was not sure how she felt about him, but he was sure of his own feelings.

The next couple of days went by in preparation for Christmas. Daniel helped his uncle with the shopping and decorating the house and the restaurant. On Christmas day, both prepared the meal together and had a late lunch. In the evening, they went fishing in the sea.

After setting down their fishing gears on the pier, David started to hook up the line. Daniel did not bother to prepare his fishing line. Instead, he walked towards the edge of the pier. Staring at the water, he inhaled deeply. The rhythmic splashing of the waves on the rocks reminded him of the day he had spent with Maya at the beach.

David had to call him again to get his attention.

"You okay, my boy?" he asked when Daniel turned around.

"Yeah." Daniel shrugged.

David smiled slightly and continued his work. He had noticed the change in Daniel's behavior and wondered what might be bothering him. He threw the bait into the water and waited for the catch. He looked towards his nephew who was lost in his own world and thought it was better not to disturb him.

Daniel was thinking how wonderful it would have been if Maya was in the same city. He would have invited her over for the Christmas dinner. They would have had a lovely time together, but she was far away. He had found interest in one girl after all and she had to be from a different city. He sighed, not realizing he was doing it, but David noticed.

David had caught a few small and one large fish. Even the large catch did not excite Daniel, so David thought it was time to go home.

David cleaned the fish and marinated them with salt, pepper and lemon, then put them in the oven to cook. While he was working on the fish, Daniel found some greens for the side dish. He washed the lettuce and diced the cucumber into small pieces. Then he cut some tomatoes and onions. He sprinkled salt and pepper over the salad and drizzled some lemon juice then mixed it all up.

When the fish was ready, David took it out from the oven and placed it on the dining table. They had some chicken left over from the lunch. Daniel grabbed two bottles of chilled beer from the fridge, then they both sat down for dinner.

David raised his bottle and said, "Happy Christmas."

"Happy Christmas!" Daniel raised his bottle too.

They talked about various things throughout the dinner. David went on to explain what was happening at the restaurant. He asked Daniel about the sites in Perth he was considering. Daniel gave all the details he had collected of each site.

"And did you meet the girl?" David asked casually.

"What girl?" Daniel was caught off guard with the question.

"The one you went to see. Did you meet her?" David raised his brows and smiled at him.

"Umm, yeah." Daniel was shy. "But how did you know?" he asked him.

"Come on, my boy, it wasn't that hard to figure out. I am an experienced man." David winked at him.

"That you are." Daniel agreed with him.

"Now, can I have more details please?" David said as he rose to get another two bottles of beer.

"Her name is Maya," Daniel started to talk softly.

He told David how he had met her and what made him go see her again. He told him about all his meetings with her and how he had spent the whole day with her at the beach.

David was listening intently, enjoying every bit. "So, you two like each other a lot," he said.

"I do. But I am not sure about her," Daniel said.

"You silly duffer, she wouldn't spend all that time with you and enjoy it if she didn't like you," David said simply, sipping his beer.

"You think so?" Daniel pressed his hands on the table and leaned forward.

"Yep!" David nodded his head, then added, "I'm an experienced man."

A smile spread across Daniel's lips and a new hope twinkled in his eyes.

They kept talking about love and life as the night rolled on.

Sixteen

Maya was quiet at work and seemed to be lost in her thoughts most of the time. She could hear Jane's voice in her head saying that it all meant nothing, and Maya had to move on. Did it all mean nothing? Maya kept asking herself.

Daniel did say that he came to Perth on his uncle's request. It seemed that they had met by coincidence, but then how was he able to give her the lost scarf? His motive for his Perth visit was not just limited to the site survey for his uncle's restaurant. He did have a plan to meet her which meant he had made an effort to see her. But why?

He must have been interested in her after their first meeting in the pub. And from these last few days she spent with him, she could tell that he liked her a lot. And she liked him too. No matter where he was, no matter when they were going to meet again, she was going to keep those memories alive. She couldn't just let go like her mother had said.

Daniel finished his college after a few months. He started to apply for jobs while working at his uncle's restaurant. He was good in the kitchen and helped the chefs when the restaurant was busy. He would fill in as a waiter when one of them didn't show up. After closing at night, he would help David with the accounts.

Daniel got a job within a month as an assistant sparky in a company. He had to work under the supervision of his seniors. His first project was to re-wire a house that was damaged in a fire. He worked with the others in a team, learning from them.

When he received his first payment, he took David out to celebrate. After having dinner in a fancy restaurant, they ended up in a local bar.

David was very happy for him. "Good on ya, my boy," he said, raising his glass.

Daniel smiled and raised his glass too. "Cheers," he said. They drank and talked for a long time.

Daniel was smart and hard working. His seniors were impressed with him and soon he was working on new sites as a lead sparky. He would be busy throughout the day and at night when he went to bed, he would think about Maya. He wondered what she might have thought after their last encounter. She wasn't mad at him for kissing her, but she wasn't excited either.

He wanted to see her and tell her about his feelings.

He decided to go to Perth again, this time only to meet her. He took two days leave from his work and got on an early flight on a Thursday morning. He was going to see her after almost eight months.

It was past afternoon when he reached Perth. He checked into the same hotel and was out as soon as he could. The clock was about to strike five, so he hurried towards the city centre, hoping to catch Maya on her way home from her work.

He waited at the corner of the road, well hidden from the oncoming crowd, focusing on the café door. People were coming out of the café which meant it wasn't closed yet. The roads were getting crowded as everyone was returning home from their work.

After waiting for about half an hour, he saw Gloria step out of the café and behind her was Maya. His heart started to beat faster. Gloria was talking and Maya was listening to her with a smile on her lips. They walked together up to the corner and then parted ways.

Maya was alone, walking slowly towards her home. Daniel started to follow her at a distance as he wanted to stay hidden until they were away from the city crowd. Maya was in no hurry. She was talking small steps, observing people around her, enjoying the late August weather. They were at halfway between the city centre and her house. The crowd had thinned; there were fewer people on the road. Daniel increased his pace. When he was a few feet behind her, he called her.

"Maya," he said softly, but loud enough for her to hear.

Maya stopped abruptly and turned around. She gasped when she saw him, her eyes widened, and her mouth opened. She covered her mouth with both her hands. It felt like a dream, but she knew it was not. He was here, in front of her, calling out her name.

Daniel stood there smiling at her, not sure whether to hug her or kiss her or to scoop her up.

"Daniel," she said finally. She rushed towards him and threw her arms around his neck. He wrapped his arms around her waist and lifted her up.

"Oh Daniel!" Maya was sobbing gently.

Daniel put her down and pushed himself away to look at her. She had tears rolling down her cheeks. He cupped her face in his hands and wiped the tears away with his thumb.

"Hey, it's okay," he said as softly as he could. It broke his heart to see her in tears.

She put her hands over his and their eyes locked. Daniel started to lower his head slowly, his eyes travelling from her eyes to her lips. He stopped midway, looked into her eyes again, searching for her approval. Maya lifted her head towards his and their lips met. Daniel could feel her shudder a bit as he kissed her gently, cupping her face in his hands. Maya closed her eyes and let herself be lost in his arms, caressing his hair and kissing him softly. They felt like the world had stopped for them.

Finally, they pulled away, and both had no idea how long they had been standing there, naïve to the stares of the few passersby.

"I am so glad to see you." Maya smiled sweetly.

"Me too," Daniel said.

They started to walk towards Maya's home. Both couldn't stop smiling.

"How have you been doing?" he asked her.

"Good and you?" she asked him.

"All good. I've finished my college and now I am working in a company," he said.

"Wow, that's great." Maya smiled, looking at him. Her happiness for him was obvious.

They walked in silence for some time. Maya stopped at the corner before her house.

"I would love to invite you in but I'm not sure how my mom would react." She went on to explain, "Last time, I told her about you, and she was not that happy."

"That's okay." He smiled.

Maya was glad that he understood.

"Can you take a day off tomorrow from work?" Daniel asked her.

"I will ask Wendy in the morning," she replied.

They were holding hands, and both didn't want to part ways, but she had to go home.

"See you tomorrow then." Maya was excited already for the next day.

"Yeah." He squeezed her hand gently.

Maya kissed him on his cheeks and started towards her home. Daniel smiled and headed towards the hotel, feeling pleased.

Both were excited for the next day. It had been so long that Maya had almost given up hope to see him again. It had been such a pleasant surprise to see him today and she couldn't wait for tomorrow.

Daniel was over the moon and couldn't stop smiling. All these times he was worried if Maya was upset with him, but he was wrong. The way she rushed into his arms when she saw him cleared all his doubts.

The following morning, Maya was up earlier than usual. After a quick shower, she changed into a lovely pink blouse and a skirt. Her mom was still in bed when she sneaked out of the front door. She almost jogged on the way to café so that she could reach Wendy early and talk with her about taking the day off. She must have reached half the way when she saw him standing at the side of the road. He had a big grin on his face when he saw her.

"Good morning," he said, approaching her.

"What are you doing here at this hour? It's too early." Maya was shaking her head in disbelief.

"Couldn't stay at the hotel." He shrugged. "Was missing you." He kissed her gently on her lips.

"You couldn't wait till lunch?" she smiled sweetly.

Daniel shook his head.

"So, what's the plan for today?" Maya asked him as they walked towards the café.

"My plan is to spend the whole day with you," Daniel replied simply to which Maya giggled.

"Right," she said.

They stopped a few blocks away from the café.

"Let me talk to Wendy first. I'll see you in a bit," Maya said and marched towards the café, leaving him standing behind.

Seventeen

Wendy had just opened the café when Maya arrived.

"Morning Wendy," Maya greeted her.

"Morning love, you're a bit early today," Wendy said.

"Yeah. Something came up and I need to take a leave today if you don't mind," Maya said in an anxious voice.

"Is everything alright?" Wendy looked concerned.

"Everything is fine, it's just that I need to sort out some stuffs." Maya was finding it hard to make an excuse.

"That's okay, but can you wait till Gloria comes in?" Wendy requested.

"Sure," Maya said, but was thinking about Daniel. He would have to wait for some time, she thought, because Gloria was hardly ever on time.

She started to arrange the tables and chairs; her eyes fixated at the doors, waiting for Gloria to arrive. Bob and Brenton had arrived and were in the kitchen. Customers had started to come in and Maya was busy serving them. It had been more than an hour already.

Poor Daniel, she thought.

It must have been almost two hours when finally, Gloria showed up. While she was chatting with Wendy, Maya went into the change room and got ready.

"What are you up to?" Gloria asked her as she entered the change room.

"You are on your own today, have fun." Maya kissed her on her cheeks as she walked out, leaving Gloria stunned.

She waved at Wendy as she hurried out of the door, not wanting to waste another minute. She did not even say a word to Wendy, who found that unusual. She went to the spot where she had left Daniel, but he wasn't there. She looked around but couldn't see him anywhere.

He must have been tired of waiting, she thought.

"Hey!" She heard him and turned around to find him holding a coffee in his hand. "I went to grab a coffee," he said.

"I am so sorry to keep you waiting. I had to wait until Gloria showed up," Maya explained.

"No worries. Not your fault," he said, "How about a breakfast?"

They walked a few blocks ahead and entered one of the cafés. Maya ordered toast and eggs and a coffee for herself. Daniel went for a chicken sandwich.

"Hmm that's good," he said, after taking a bite. "So, what do you want to do today?" he asked Maya who was munching on her toast.

"Spend the day with you," Maya said with a wide grin.

Daniel was amused. "I'd love that," he said.

After finishing their food, they headed out of the café. They walked a bit and reached a spot from where they could see Perth city and the Swan River.

"It's a beautiful view," Daniel said, observing the city.

"It is," Maya agreed.

Daniel put his hand on Maya's shoulder. She touched his fingers and looked up into his eyes. Their lips touched for a moment, then they continued to watch over the city. Both had smiles on their faces, their eyes beaming with happiness.

"Would you like to walk around?" Maya asked, after a while.

"Let's go," Daniel said, and they walked towards a small park nearby, holding hands. Maya was stiff suddenly, she let go of his hand and marched ahead.

"Sophie!" she was shouting and waving at someone ahead. He saw a lady pushing a stroller.

"Maya! what a pleasant surprise!" Sophie hugged Maya. She looked excited to meet her.

"How are you?" Maya asked her.

"I'm good. You haven't met little Kevin, have you?" Sophie proudly looked towards her baby. He was sleeping peacefully in the stroller.

"Oh! He is beautiful, just like you," Maya said, adoring the little baby.

There was a lady standing behind Sophie, holding bags and an umbrella. She must be the maid, Maya thought. Daniel had caught up with her and was now standing beside her.

"This is Sophie, and this is my friend, Daniel," Maya introduced them. She didn't want to give much detail about him as she wasn't close to Sophie anymore.

"Nice to meet you," Daniel said with a smile.

"Glad to meet you too," Sophie smiled at him.

Sophie and Maya walked together while Daniel offered to push the stroller and walk behind them.

"How is George?" Maya asked.

"He is good, busy with his work," Sophie said. They chatted all along the way, Sophie doing most of the talking. Maya noticed that she hadn't changed much and could tell that she was very happy with her life.

"What about you? Have you met anyone?" Sophie asked in an excited voice.

"Me? No!" Maya waved her hand.

"He is not bad," Sophie tried to tease her while looking at Daniel from the corner of her eye.

Maya rolled her eyes. "He is a friend of a friend actually," she said, and went on to explain that he was from Sydney on a visit.

"Sydney huh? That makes him even more perfect." Sophie was grinning.

"Oh, come on. Leave him now," Maya said, and they both giggled on. They kept strolling around for quite some time. Maya looked at Daniel and realized that he must be feeling bored.

"I promised him a tour around the city," Maya told Sophie, looking towards Daniel.

"Well, then go on and have fun." Sophie smiled. "It was great meeting you," she said, and hugged her.

"Yeah, I'm glad we met," Maya said.

Sophie took the stroller from Daniel. "Thank you," she said to him.

"No problem at all," he replied.

"Hope you will enjoy your stay here," Sophie said to him and waved at them as she moved on.

"I'm sorry you were left by yourself out there," Maya said to Daniel when they had parted their ways.

"That wasn't my idea of spending time with you, but it's okay, she was your friend," Daniel said.

"We were friends when we were kids. I haven't seen her since her wedding," she said.

Daniel put his arms around her shoulders, pulling her closer to him. She looked at him and smiled. They walked around, enjoying each other's company and the beautiful surrounding. The weather was just perfect with the sun shining up high, a few scattered clouds and a slow breeze.

"Do you want to go to the beach?" Maya asked, after they had spent more than an hour. She knew he enjoyed being at the beach.

"It's a bit late for the beach today, how about tomorrow?" he suggested, "We will go early and spend the whole day there."

"Okay. Where do you want to go now?" Maya asked.

"Let's just stay by the riverside," Daniel said.

Maya loved the idea. She wouldn't want to be anywhere else. They walked along the bank for some time then sat on a bench facing the river. Maya rested her head on his shoulder. She remembered how she used to come here and watch other couples walk hand in hand.

It was getting cloudy; the cool breeze gave Maya chills and she shuddered a bit. Daniel wrapped his arms around her.

"Are you feeling cold?" Daniel asked when he felt that her arms were cooler than his.

"You are keeping me warm," she said, snuggling in his arms. "This feels nice," she murmured.

"Hmmm." He kissed on her forehead.

"Do you need to be home early?" he asked, noticing the time on his watch.

"I am usually late on Fridays." She smiled at him. "The café is busy till late and sometimes I come here to spend the evening."

"Perfect!" Daniel relaxed a bit, stretching his legs.

"Has your uncle decided yet about moving here?" she asked him.

"Yes. Maybe by the end of this year. He wants to start the restaurant here from next year," Daniel explained.

"And what about you?" she asked.

"I will have to stay by myself, I guess. I have just started the work you know," he said.

Maya nodded. "Has he made up his mind about the spot?" she asked again.

"He is considering Fremantle for now. It's a port, so he says it will be busy most of the time and good for his business." Daniel was elaborating but Maya wasn't listening to any of it.

When he first mentioned the name, she felt like he had unlocked her memories that she had kept buried inside her for a long time. She remembered her mom mentioning the name when her father had left.

Suddenly, she noticed that Daniel was saying something to her.

"Have you been there?" he was asking her.

"No." Maya was stern.

She was serious all of a sudden, but Daniel didn't question her further although it made him anxious.

Eighteen

The sun had set, and it was getting dark. There were a few streetlights to illuminate the path. Maya looked up into the sky; a few stars were twinkling, and she smiled.

Daniel looked at her. He could see a twinkle in her eyes, her face was glowing under the streetlight, and she looked innocently happy, almost like a child. He followed her gaze up towards the sky.

"I love watching them," Maya said, "Beautiful, mysterious, twinkly dots scattered in the sky."

Daniel smiled.

"You might find it weird, but I spend some time at nights, talking to them." Maya was going on, still looking up to the sky, "They have been my friends forever. I share my feelings with them. If I wish for something, I tell them, believing that they are listening to me."

Daniel was staring at her, finding it hard to believe. He was thinking, was it just a coincidence that they had met, or was it meant to be? How is it possible? Growing up, he used to sit out at nights and stare at the stars, imagining things, and now he was sitting with this girl, who was telling him that she used to do the same.

"I love you," Daniel said, in a low voice.

"What?" Maya stared at him, not sure if she had heard him right.

"I love you, Maya." He was loud and clear this time.

She opened her mouth, but no words came out. She looked into his eyes and she could tell that he was serious. One hand still on her shoulder, he cupped her face with the other hand and leaned forward to kiss her. She closed her eyes, breathed in deeply, lifted her hand and rested it on his chest. Their lips met, feeling warm against each other's. Maya parted her lips to welcome him. Her mouth was soft and moist. They were lost in each other's embrace.

"And I love you," Maya said, gazing into his eyes.

Daniel's eyes twinkled and he gave the sweetest smile she had ever seen. They spent some more time together observing the surroundings.

"You should go home now," Daniel said, "It's getting late."

"Yeah," she whispered.

They both got up and started towards her home, he still had his arms around her.

"Beach tomorrow?" Daniel asked.

"Sure," Maya replied.

"What time will I see you?" he asked again.

"It's Saturday. I can only leave after breakfast with my mom," Maya said, "I'll meet you by the station around noon."

"Okay," he nodded.

She was a bit late than usual for arriving home. Her mom was in the kitchen, waiting for her.

"Was it very busy today? You must be very tired," Jane said as Maya entered the house.

"Hey, mom!" Maya went to hug Jane. She hadn't been at work all day and her mother was worried about her being tired. She felt guilty for hiding the truth.

They had dinner, talking about the usual things. Jane said that she had plans for the next day. She was going to the bakery and visiting a few friends which meant she would be busy throughout the day. Maya felt relieved. She could sneak out after Jane left and be back before she arrived home. That way, she wouldn't have to make up a story about where she had been all day.

The sound of a heavy downpour woke Maya up early on Saturday. "What a day!" She sighed heavily. She was looking forward to going to the beach and having a good time like the last trip, but the weather was not in her favor today. She kept staring at the ceiling, listening to the sound of the rain, and thinking about Daniel.

Wouldn't it be wonderful to wake up in someone's arms on a morning like this? she thought. She snuggled up under her covers, trying to feel the warmth. She closed her eyes and was about to doze off again when her mom entered the room with a steaming cup in her hand.

"Looks like it's going to rain all day. Good for you, you can snuggle in bed all day," Jane said as she put the cup next to her bed. "I'll be in the kitchen," she said as she left the room.

Maya kept looking out of the window in hopes to see the sky clearing out, but it was covered in dark clouds.

She had to meet Daniel anyway. Though he hadn't said anything, she knew that he was not going to stay for long.

After a quick shower, she had breakfast with Jane. Maya offered to do the dishes so that Jane could get ready for her day out. Maya was still in the kitchen when her mom was heading out.

"Bye, honey!" she called from the front door.

"Bye, mom!" Maya shouted from the kitchen. She checked on the clock hanging on the wall. She had about an hour before she met Daniel.

Maya scanned through her closet, wondering what to wear. They were not going to the beach in this weather for sure. She went for a pair of black jeans and a blue silk blouse. She moved the curtain to the side and looked through the window. Even from inside her room, she could feel the chills. Not wanting to take any chances, she pulled out a light sweater from her closet.

After changing her clothes, she did her hair and put on a light makeup. When she was satisfied with her look, she grabbed an umbrella and walked out into the rain. She held the umbrella with one hand and held the other arm across her chest to keep herself warm. She was glad that she had the sweater on.

Daniel was there when she reached the station. He had a big umbrella with him and a big smile on his face when he saw her.

"Hey!" he said, walking towards her.

"Hey!" She smiled.

He pulled her under his umbrella and closed hers.

"Are you cold?" he asked.

"It is cold," Maya said. She was getting the chills.

Daniel wrapped his arm around her and pulled her closer. "Better?" he asked, looking at her.

Maya nodded with a smile. That did feel better. He planted a kiss on her forehead.

"Now that the beach is cancelled, where do we go?" Maya asked, walking out of the station. She sneezed once and then again.

"Are you feeling okay?" Daniel noticed her nose tip was getting color and her eyes were watery.

"Yeah, I'm fine," she said, and sneezed a couple of times.

"I know where we are going," Daniel said, and led the way.

Maya wondered where he was planning to go. After a few minutes' walk, she realized that they were heading towards the hotel and she stopped abruptly.

"Why are we going to your hotel?" she asked.

"Because it's raining, we don't have a specific plan, and you are not feeling good," Daniel said.

"I am feeling very good." She sneezed as soon as she said it.

"Yeah, I can see that," he said, "Now come on, you need to be warm," he tugged her.

Maya walked reluctantly though she thought being somewhere dry would be great right now. They entered the hotel, walked through the lobby, then into the elevator. Daniel punched some keys and the doors closed. When the doors opened again, they were in a corridor with doors on either side. Daniel stopped in front of one of the doors, reached into his pocket for the keys and opened the door.

They entered the room which had a single bed on one side. The room was small with one sofa and a coffee table on the other side. She went to sit on the sofa. Daniel pulled a blanket from the bed and gave it to her. She wrapped it around her and felt the warmth of it against her body.

"Thank you," she said.

"Lie down for a while, you will feel better," Daniel said, pointing towards the bed.

"I am feeling better already," she said, slipping her shoes off and bringing her legs up to cover them with the blanket. She was avoiding eye contact with him.

Daniel noticed her uneasiness, so he picked up a newspaper from the table and went to sit at the end of the bed. He began to scan through the pages, pretending to avoid her.

"What's in the paper?" Maya asked after a while.

"Usual stuffs," Daniel replied without looking at her.

Maya had no idea what the usual stuffs were; she never read the papers. She tilted her head upwards and rested it on the sofa, then closed her eyes.

Daniel watched her from the corner of his eyes. He put the paper aside and got up on his feet. Maya opened her eyes when she heard him move.

"I'll be back in a moment," he said, and went out of the room locking the door behind him.

Maya was confused. Where could he be going, leaving her alone in the room?

She leaned her head back again; her eyelids were heavy, and she was breathing heavily within a minute.

Nineteen

The door swung open after a click and Daniel stepped in holding a tray in his hands. When he saw that Maya had dozed off, he slowly put the tray on the table so as not to make any sound. He had gone to get something hot for her to drink and was back with coffee and soup, not sure what she would prefer.

He looked at her sleeping peacefully. He covered the soup mug and the coffee cup with saucers. He then picked up his coffee and went to sit on the bed again. Sipping his coffee slowly, he kept watching her.

How wonderful it would be if this was their own room and they lived together, he thought. He would get to see her sleep like this every morning. He wanted to hold her in his arms as she slept, breathe her soft hair, feel her heartbeat and the warmth of her body. Maya was sleeping but he was dreaming about their future together.

She stirred in her sleep and a lock of her hair fell on her face. He stood up and walked towards her. He put the empty cup on the table and leaned down towards her.

He carefully moved her hair and kissed her gently on her forehead.

"I love you," he whispered.

Maya moved a bit, and Daniel recoiled back. He then went to the window and looked outside. The sky had started to clear out, but it was still drizzling. The clock ticked on and he felt heavier as the day passed by. He hadn't mentioned it to Maya that he had to leave the next day to get back to his work on Monday. He was lost deep in his thoughts, and he didn't notice the stir behind him.

Maya had woken up feeling much better. She looked around and saw him standing by the window, staring out.

"Did I sleep for long?" she asked, clearing her throat.

Daniel turned around and smiled at her. "How are you feeling now?" he asked her.

"A lot better," she replied.

"I went to get you something hot to drink." He checked on the soup. "It's not that hot now. I will get another one."

Maya reached forward and felt the mug. "It's still warm," she said, and took the mug in her hands.

"Are you sure?" he asked.

Maya nodded and sipped the soup. "Hmm, it's good. Thank you," she said. She finished her soup, then pulled away the blanket that was wrapped around her.

"Can I use the bathroom?" she asked.

"Sure, that way." Daniel pointed towards a door.

Maya walked through it and entered a small bathroom. She saw herself in the mirror and felt embarrassed. I look terrible, she thought. Her hair was a mess, eyes were puffed, and she looked tired. She washed her face with cold water and patted it dry with a towel, then managed to comb her hair with her fingers. She mended her sweater and jeans. The hem of her jeans was still wet from the rain. Glancing at the mirror once again, she went out into the room.

Daniel was standing by the window again. Maya went to stand beside him.

"The rain ruined your idea about having fun on the beach and I ruined the idea of having a good time by catching a cold." She sighed.

"What are you talking about? The idea was to spend time with you," he said, touching her shoulder.

"Not a 'sick' me," she said.

Daniel turned towards her and held her both hands in his. "You have no idea what a good time I had watching you sleep," he said.

"What?" Maya felt shy.

Daniel laughed lightly and hugged her, "I was worried that you would feel worse. But you are better now, thank God."

Maya looked at him and smiled. He lowered his head to kiss her, but she turned away and his lips touched her cheek.

"I don't want you to share my germs," she said.

"But you said you were feeling better," he complained.

"I am feeling better but not healed completely," she argued.

"I am relieved that you are getting better otherwise it would be hard to leave you behind in that state," he hugged her tightly.

Maya smiled and snuggled on his chest. It felt good that he cared for her so much. It took her a moment to realize what he had just said. "What do you mean?" she asked, pulling herself away from his arms.

"I am sorry, but I have to leave tomorrow." Daniel tried to hold her hands, but she jerked away.

"And when were you going to tell me?" Maya was upset.

"I have to be at work on Monday. I've just started so couldn't take more days off," he tried to explain.

"Then why did you even bother to come here?" She turned away from him.

Daniel was stunned by her remark; he was very hurt. "You know why, because I had to see you, I wanted to see you," he said in a very low voice, "Please don't be mad."

Maya didn't say anything, she walked to the sofa and sat on it. She had tears in her eyes and didn't want him to see them.

"I should have told you earlier, I am sorry," he said from behind her. "Maya, please say something," Daniel was begging her.

"My mom was right. I should have listened to her. I should have forgotten about you and moved on." Maya couldn't hold her tears back anymore and let them flow down her cheeks.

"No, no, don't say that." Daniel came around and kneeled in front of her. "I love you, and I know you love me too," he said.

"But what's the point when we can't be together?" Maya sobbed. That was what her mother had said to her before.

"We can make it work out, we will find a way," he was trying to convince her.

But she was shaking her head while wiping her tears with a tissue. Daniel put his hand on her knees. Inhaling deeply, he said, "Come with me."

Maya looked at him in disbelief. "I can't," she whispered.

"Why not?" he asked.

"I can't leave my mom," she replied, and stood up. "I know what it feels like when someone leaves you, we have been through it once and I don't want her to go through it again."

Daniel remembered her once telling him that her father had left them when she was a kid.

Suddenly Maya found it hard to breathe, it felt like she was suffocating in the room. "I need to get out of here, I have to go," she said.

"No! Please." Daniel stood up. "Don't go," he begged, holding her hand.

"If you can go whenever you want, then why can't I?" She pulled her hand free from his grasp and looked towards the door.

"Don't leave like this." He stood between her and the door. "What we have is beautiful, let's not end it like this." Maya was shaking her head. "I'll find a way, I will make a way, I promise." He was trying his best to make her believe in him.

She wanted to believe in him, but for now, she had to be away from him. "I have to go now. Mom doesn't know that I am away. I want to be home when she returns," Maya said, looking at the floor.

Daniel's heart got heavy. He stepped aside, looking sad. "I'll see you again." He wanted to sound hopeful.

Maya looked up at him, tears rolled down her cheeks. She had a question in her eyes, 'when?' but didn't say a word. She went to the door, opened it and walked out without looking back. The door closed behind her. She didn't see the tears dropping down from his eyes.

Daniel stood staring at the closed door for a long time, letting the tears fall. He was hurt and even angry at himself for letting all this happen. He was also scared that he might have lost her. He wanted to run after her and stop her, but he had seen the look in her eyes and didn't have the courage to face her. He went to sit on the bed, lowered his head and rested it in his hands. He shut his eyes. What have I done? he thought and shook his head.

When Maya reached home, Jane was not there which made her feel a bit relieved, at least she did not have to explain to her about where she had been. She changed quickly and jumped into her bed, then covered her face with a pillow. She sobbed, letting out all her frustration and anger. She asked herself, why couldn't her life be simpler? Why couldn't she have happiness like other people did? She was angry with her life for being harsh on her.

She wasn't mad at Daniel; how could she be? He had come all the way to see her, more than once. He had even asked her to come with him, what more could he offer than that?

It was her life that was complicated. She had found someone who loved her and more important than that, she loved him. But she loved her mom too, and she couldn't leave her behind and move to another city to be with him. Her mother had been through a lot and sacrificed so much for her. Her mother hadn't abandoned her like her father had. And now she wouldn't abandon her either. She wouldn't leave Perth.

Twenty

"I'm home!" Jane called as she entered the house.

"In here, mom," Maya answered in a hoarse voice from her room.

Jane sensed something was wrong and went to her daughter's room. Maya was lying down, facing the other way. "Have you been in bed all day?" Jane asked her. When she turned around, she almost gasped. "Oh my god, what happened? Are you not feeling well?" She put her palm on Maya's forehead and cheeks. Maya's eyes were puffed, and her face was red.

"I think I have got a cold," Maya said.

"Oh… it must be the weather that got you," Jane said, "I'll make you some soup, it will help you feel better." Jane tucked the blanket properly over Maya and got up to go to the kitchen.

"Mom," Maya said.

"Yes, darling?" Jane stooped over a bit.

"I love you," Maya said in a thin voice.

"I love you too, honey." She kissed her on her forehead and smiled. "You rest, okay? I'll be back with the soup." Jane went out of the room. Maya shut her eyes and inhaled deeply.

"I love you, mom," she repeated in a whisper.

Gloria had noticed the change in Maya. She had stopped smiling, no small chit chats like they used to have, no jokes, no laughs. Maya was quiet again just like she was when she had first met her. Gloria tried to talk but Maya avoided her, saying it was nothing. One day after closing the café, Gloria entered the change room and found Maya in tears.

"Will you stop saying it's nothing and tell me what's going on with you?" Gloria sat next to Maya and put her arms around her.

Maya sobbed, wiped her tears with her hands and told her everything about Daniel. She broke down again when she told her about their last meeting at the hotel.

For the first time, Maya saw Gloria speechless. She just kept staring at her. "Wow!" she said after some time. "So, you and Daniel huh?"

"But it's over now." Maya shook her head.

"Why do you say that?" Gloria asked.

"He lives in Sydney," Maya said.

"So what? He did ask you to come with him, didn't he?" Gloria couldn't understand why she was so upset about it.

"I can't go. I can't leave my mom alone here." Maya sobbed again.

"Don't be silly," Gloria said, "You will have to leave her even if you marry someone who lives here."

"Yes, but then I will be here in the same city. I can see her every day, visit her and stay over whenever she needs me. That won't be possible if I go somewhere else," Maya said. Gloria didn't know what to say to that, she knew Maya was very close to her mom.

Daniel returned home with a heavy heart. David was excited to see him but when he heard what had happened, he felt sorry for him. Daniel returned to work the next day. Though he was working, he kept thinking about Maya all day. He went to his room after dinner and started to unpack the travel bag he had taken to Perth. He took out a black umbrella and held it in his hand. It was Maya's. She had forgotten about it when she had left the hotel room. From that day onwards, he used that same umbrella when he had to go out in the rain.

A couple of months had passed. Daniel went to work during the day and spent the evenings at the restaurant. He spent time with David at the restaurant and at home, but he stopped going to the bar with him. David was worried for his nephew; he had stopped enjoying his life. One night, Daniel was in the backyard, staring at the sky. David went and stood beside him.

"Why aren't you doing anything about it?" he asked Daniel.

"About what?" Daniel said without thinking.

"About you and Maya. You are not going to let it end like this, are you?" He was waving his hands as he talked.

"I tried. I asked her to come with me, but she said she can't leave her mother." Daniel looked down feeling helpless.

"A girl like that is a gem, Daniel. If she loves her mother so much, she will fill your life with love and happiness. Don't lose her." David's voice was very deep. "If she can't come to you then why don't you go to her?" He put his hand on Daniel's shoulder and squeezed a bit.

Daniel looked up at him, and David nodded his head. That night, Daniel felt a sense of relief settle on him. Giving a thought to his uncle's suggestion, he decided to leave Sydney and move to Perth. It meant he had to start over again: find a place to live and a new job. But if he could get Maya back in his life, he was ready to go through all that. He sat with David for hours to discuss about what they would do next. It was decided that Daniel would leave the following month. He would stay at Wendy's house for the initial days, and then find a place to live and a job. David would join him during Christmas and start working for the new restaurant. Until then, he would settle the business matters here in Sydney. Daniel was very excited. He couldn't wait to meet Maya and tell her everything.

Daniel arrived in Perth on a Saturday afternoon in the middle of November. He went to Wendy's house where she met him at the door with a hug. David had talked with her on phone and told her about his plan, but he had avoided saying the reason why Daniel was moving to Perth. Wendy lived alone in her house, as her husband had passed away years ago and they had no children.

She didn't see anyone after her husband's death and kept herself busy at the café. She had a cat as a companion and was more than happy to let Daniel stay in her house.

Daniel wanted to see Maya soon, but the café was closed on the weekends, so he had to wait. He had a quick shower, changed clothes, then went to help Wendy who was preparing dinner for them.

"Thanks for letting me stay. I'll find a place soon," Daniel said. Wendy was cutting vegetables.

"What nonsense, you don't have to go find a place. You can stay here as long as you want, there's plenty of room in the house," she said, waving the knife.

Daniel smiled. He was debating in his mind whether he should tell her about Maya. Then he thought it was better to wait until he met her first.

The next morning, Daniel woke up early. He couldn't see Wendy around the house and thought she must be sleeping in late on a Sunday morning. He went into the kitchen and made himself a cup of coffee. Holding the cup in his hand, he went to the front door and opened it to take a look around. He saw Wendy jogging towards the house from the main street.

"Good morning, Daniel." She waved at him.

"Good morning. I thought you were sleeping in late." Daniel smiled at her.

"I'm used to getting up early. It's good for my health, you know." She winked at him.

"Can I make you some coffee?" Daniel offered.

"I would love it but first let me take a shower." Wendy headed to her room. When she was out, her steaming coffee was resting on the dining table. "Hmm, thank you," she said, grabbing her cup.

Wendy's cat came snuggling around her feet, it was a fluffy brown and white cat. "Hey!" Wendy bent down and scooped her up. "I call her Amber," she said, kissing the cat's nose. Amber purred and made herself comfortable on Wendy's lap as she stroked her back.

"She misses me the other days when I am away and doesn't leave my side when I am home on weekends," Wendy said, cuddling Amber.

"How is the café going?" Daniel asked. He was planning to go there the next day to meet Maya.

"Oh, it's good usually, but we get caught up sometime these days since Gloria is on holiday and with just one girl serving the customers…" Wendy shook her head lightly.

"Gloria is on holiday?" Daniel repeated.

"Yeah. She has taken a couple of weeks off from work and is gone with Mark." Wendy stood up, carrying Amber over her shoulder and took her empty cup over to the sink.

"I could lend a helping hand at the café if you want." Daniel was excited already, thinking about working with Maya in the café.

"Oh, you don't need to trouble yourself." Wendy waved her hand.

"I have worked at my uncle's restaurant, so it won't be a problem for me and it's only until Gloria gets back. Besides, I will be staying at home doing nothing," Daniel persuaded.

"Okay then, if you want to, you can come with me tomorrow." Wendy smiled.

Daniel couldn't wait for the next day. He imagined the surprise look on Maya's face when she would see him in the café.

Wendy and Daniel were at the café early Monday morning. Wendy helped Daniel set the tables and chairs. Daniel went to the change room to put on an apron. He stood in front of the counter facing the entrance, pretending to wait for the customers but was hoping for Maya to walk through the doors.

Two men walked in and ordered coffee. Daniel was getting their coffee when a young lady entered and greeted Wendy, who then called Daniel over and introduced her. "This is Claire, and this is Daniel. He will be helping us until Gloria is back," Wendy said.

They exchanged their hello and Claire disappeared into the change room. Daniel stood there a bit confused. He was expecting Maya to be at the café anytime now. Just then, a few more people walked into the café, so he went to serve them. It was mid-day and there was still no sign of Maya. Daniel was getting anxious by then. He met Claire in the change room after lunch time.

"Hi," he said, clearing his throat.

"Hi there." Claire smiled at him.

"Do you know why Maya didn't come to work today?" Daniel asked her.

"I'm sorry, who?" Claire shrugged.

"Maya. She works here with Gloria," Daniel said.

"No, I haven't met her." Claire shook her head.

"How long have you been working here?" Daniel asked her in an alarmed voice.

"More than a month." With that, Claire left the room.

This can't be true, she must be confused, Daniel thought, then went to find Wendy to ask her about Maya.

"Hey, Wendy, is Maya not coming today?" He asked casually.

"She doesn't work here anymore. It's been more than a month," Wendy replied from behind the counter.

Twenty-One

"Why? What happened? I mean, did she say anything about why she was leaving?" Daniel almost stuttered as he asked Wendy about Maya. He was hoping to surprise her, but now he was the one who was surprised instead.

"Don't know. She didn't give any reason and I didn't ask," Wendy replied.

Daniel wanted to ask if Wendy knew where she might be working now, but he got the hint that she wouldn't have any clue. His mind was spinning as he worked for the rest of the day. Why did she leave this job? Where did she start to work? Where could she be right now? Gloria might know about this, he thought, but Gloria was on holiday and wouldn't be back until the end of the week. He couldn't wait that long; he had to see Maya soon. He made up his mind to go to Maya's house after closing the café.

They closed the café after five. Wendy was expecting Daniel to come home with her, but he told her that he would like to explore the city in the evening. It was just an excuse he was using to go see Maya. He almost jogged all the way up to Maya's house and was panting when he reached there. Daniel hesitated at first. He remembered how reluctant Maya was to take him home because of her mother. He waited for some time, then gathered some courage to walk up to the front door and knock on it.

No one answered. He knocked again and then again, but no one came to open the door. He started to feel restless and stepped away from the door. He walked up and down the walkway looking around, but couldn't see anyone, even in the neighborhood. He waited across the street for almost an hour and still there was no sign of anyone. A sense of fear started to settle on him slowly. What if she had moved to some other place? Daniel shook his head and he could feel the sweat forming on his forehead.

"No, no," he mumbled. She should be back home anytime now, he thought. After waiting for another thirty minutes, he decided to return. He kept looking back at the door as he walked away with a heavy heart.

"Did you have a good walk?" Wendy asked Daniel when she heard the front door open. She was reading a book on the couch with Amber curled up on her lap.

"Uh, yeah," Daniel replied in a low voice.

"You look tired. Dinner is in the fridge. Let me heat it up for you." Wendy was about to get up when Daniel stopped her.

"Thank you, but I had some food on my way, I'm full," he lied. He had lost his appetite. "If you don't mind, I would like to go to bed early." He wanted to be alone.

Wendy nodded with a smile.

Daniel rushed to his room and crashed on his bed. He was tired and so was his brain. He had been thinking a lot, thinking about Maya, thinking about where she was, thinking about the possibilities of what could have happened after he had left the last time. His head started to thump; he felt a sharp pain in his temples.

The next day after work, Daniel went to Maya's house again, knocked on the door, waited for an hour, but didn't get to see anyone. The same thing happened in the following days. Daniel was sure by now that Maya had moved to some other place. He had moved from Sydney to be with her, but she was gone, and he didn't know where. His only hope to find her was Gloria, so he waited intently for her to return from holiday.

She didn't see him on the first day as she had returned home late that evening. On the second day, at the bend on the street before her house, she stopped dead in her tracks. He was facing the other way, but she recognized him right away.

Maya jerked backwards and hid herself behind the bushes. She thought, what was he doing here? Then again, of course he was here to see her. He must have been to the café and not finding her there, he must have come to her house. For one moment, she wanted to rush towards him and embrace him in her arms but then she stopped herself, remembering their last day at the hotel. She did not want them to go over the same thing again. It was painful.

She kept hiding until Daniel went away. Tears were rolling down her cheeks as she watched him walk down the street. From that day onwards, Maya became more alert, watching every corner of the roads, inspecting the walkway before entering or leaving the house.

Maya had found it hard to go to the café every day after what happened. She was trying to get over Daniel, but the café made her memories of him more vivid. One night, Jane told her over dinner that Sally would not be able to work at the bakery anymore and they were looking for someone to replace her. Maya thought that was her chance, so she told Jane that she would love to work at the bakery. When it was fixed for her to work there, Maya informed Wendy, who said it was okay with her.

Gloria had tried to convince her to stay. Maya told her that she did not want to work as a waitress anymore, but they both knew the reason why Maya wanted to leave the café.

"Hey, I am not going anywhere. You can come see me whenever you want." Maya tried to cheer her up.

"Yeah, but it won't be the same here without you." Gloria's voice was low.

Maya had started to work at the bakery. She had to do what Sally used to do: greet the customers, give them what they ordered and handle the payments. She stood behind the counter all day, occasionally sitting on a chair when there was no one around. She felt it was a lot better here than at the café, especially because she wasn't constantly reminded of Daniel.

Gloria had come to visit her after a couple of weeks.

"You look better," she had said, after hugging Maya and inspecting her closely.

"I am feeling better," Maya had smiled broadly.

"So, you seeing anyone?" Gloria had teased her.

"What? No," Maya had replied.

"You are still hung up on him, aren't you?" Gloria had sighed.

Maya had said that she would get over him, it would take time, but she would. Later on, she realized that it wasn't going to happen. She loved him, he was her first love, maybe her only love ever. They may never be together again, but she would always love him. She was getting along just fine with that thought, but there he was again to make things hard for her. She just hoped that Daniel would return to Sydney soon.

On Monday morning, Wendy said to Daniel that he did not need to come to the café as Gloria was returning to work that day, but Daniel insisted on going with her. He said he wanted to catch up with Gloria.

Claire was on time, but Gloria as usual was late by an hour or so. She was chatting eagerly with Wendy when Daniel came out of the kitchen.

"Hey, Gloria, how was your holiday?" Daniel was putting in an effort to sound normal.

"Hey! Daniel!" Gloria was very surprised to see him in the café. "I didn't know you were working here." She tried to look pleased, but was curious, trying to figure out what he was doing there.

Daniel could sense that Gloria was not very comfortable seeing him. Had Maya told her about them? He guessed that she might have. They were busy serving customers for another few hours. When Daniel spotted Gloria entering the change room, he followed her in there. Gloria just smiled when he walked in.

"Where is Maya?" he blurted out.

Gloria kept staring at him with wide eyes. She wasn't sure what to say.

"You know about us, don't you?" Daniel eyed her closely.

Gloria nodded her head, still staring at him.

"I have come to see her, but she is gone. Can you tell me where I can find her?" he begged.

"Why do you want to see her when it's over between you two? She told me everything. I know it's not your fault, but you can't blame her either. She is trying to get over you, so don't make it harder for her. I don't think you should see her." Gloria kept on babbling.

Daniel held her arms and shook her a bit. "Gloria, listen to me. I have moved to Perth to be with her. You need to help me here," he said.

Gloria blinked her eyes a couple of times, trying to be sure if she had heard him right. Daniel nodded his head in confirmation.

"I think you should see her!" Gloria cried. She threw her arms around his neck and hugged him. "I'll take you to her, come on." She took her apron off and Daniel did the same.

It was past lunch time so there was less of a crowd in the café. Gloria was holding Daniel's hand and dragging him along. "Wendy, we got to go, I will explain later!" Gloria shouted as they both ran out of the café, leaving Wendy stunned behind the counter. They kept running till they reached Gloria's car.

"Hop in!" Gloria shouted. She was more excited than Daniel and couldn't stop grinning. On the way, she kept talking. She told Daniel that Maya had left because the café reminded her of him.

"She says she is doing fine, but I can tell that she is not. She is so in love with you. Wait until she sees you." Gloria chuckled.

Daniel was smiling too. He was so relieved and happy that he was going to see her. Last week, he had come to realize how much he was in love with her. The fear of losing her had almost killed him. "You are my savior, thank you so much," he said to Gloria.

"My pleasure," Gloria beamed.

Gloria stopped her car in a carpark in front of the bakery. She jumped out of the car and signaled Daniel to get out too. He got out of the car slowly, his heart was racing. He followed Gloria as she rushed in through the door.

Maya was behind the counter when Gloria entered and waved at her with a wide grin. Maya was pleased to see her. She came around the counter and hugged her.

"It's so good to see you, how have you been?" Maya asked her.

"I am good, but you, my dear, are going to be way better." Gloria cupped Maya's cheeks in her hands as she said so.

Maya smiled at her. She was amused by her behavior. The door opened and Maya looked towards it, expecting a customer. Her smile faded away and the color drained from her face when she saw Daniel enter. He stepped inside and stood by the door; his eyes fixed on her.

Maya looked at Gloria. "What did I tell you?" she whispered in frustration.

"Before you get angry at me, you have to listen to what he has to say." Gloria looked towards Daniel in admiration. Maya turned towards Daniel.

He was fixed on his spot. "You have something that belongs to me," he said, clearing his throat.

Maya tried to think of anything but couldn't remember keeping something that belonged to him. Gloria raised her brows, not understanding what he was saying.

"And I want you to keep it," Daniel added.

"Sorry, I don't think I have anything," Maya said.

"Yes, you have," he said, "You have my heart."

Twenty-Two

Maya almost choked as she was trying hard to hold back her tears. They kept looking at each other for a long time.

"Daniel, we talked about this," Maya said softly.

Gloria turned to Maya and said, "He has moved here from Sydney to be with you." She then turned to Daniel, "Sorry, I couldn't hold it in any longer."

Maya looked at Gloria and then at Daniel. She was trying to say, 'what is she talking about?' and Daniel understood her. He nodded his head, then smiled for the first time after being there. He took steps towards her slowly while Maya was unable to move.

"W-what, but why?" She found herself short of words.

Daniel held her hands and gazed into her eyes, "You couldn't come with me, and I couldn't live a life without you in it. I love you, Maya." He leaned forward and kissed her, then hugged her tightly.

"I love you." Maya sobbed lightly against his chest.

"I love you both!" Gloria shouted, and hugged them both at the same time. They all had smiles on their faces and happiness in their hearts.

"Okay, my job here is done and I need to get back to the café. I guess you would like to stay here," Gloria teased Daniel, who smiled with a nod. Gloria took off, leaving behind the two in each other's embrace.

"You had to leave your job." Maya felt bad about it.

"I can find another job, but I could have never found anyone like you." Daniel kissed on her forehead. "How's your mother? Does she still hate me?" he asked.

"She doesn't hate you. She was just concerned about me. She didn't want me to get into a relationship that led nowhere," Maya tried to explain.

"So, she wouldn't have any problem if I married her daughter?" He had a serious look in his eyes. Maya was speechless, she stared at him with wide eyes.

Daniel held her hands, "I didn't move here just to see you, I want to live the rest of my life with you. Please marry me," he begged, squeezing her hands.

Maya couldn't speak, tears welled up in her eyes. She nodded her head and threw her arms around him. After five o'clock, Maya closed the bakery and they walked out holding hands.

"Want to go somewhere?" Daniel asked.

Maya thought for a while. "Why don't we go to my home? You can meet my mom," she said.

"Oh, I don't think so," Daniel hesitated.

"Why not? We have to tell her, and I want to do it together with you." Maya started to pull his hand.

Daniel was reluctant but he knew she was right, he had to meet her mother someday, so why not now.

They were sitting around the dining table. Each had a different expression on their face. Maya was smiling as she was excited. Daniel was nervous and he was looking down at his hands most of the time. Jane had mixed feelings. She was surprised at first when Maya came home with a handsome young man. She was a bit annoyed when Maya introduced him as Daniel. And now she gave a perplexed look to both of them when Maya announced that they wanted to get married.

"So, you are telling me that you are staying at someone else's place and you don't have a job and yet you want to get married." Jane sounded stern and her eyes were fixed on Daniel.

"Mom, he just moved here, for me, isn't that enough?" Maya tried to defend him.

"I appreciate that, but what is he going to do now?" Jane asked.

"Mom," Maya tried to say something, but Daniel interrupted her, "Your mother is right, I need to sort things out first, find a job and get a place to live in," he said.

"That's more sensible." Jane forced a smile.

There was a long silence in the room, then Daniel stood up slowly, "I should get going, it was nice to meet you," he said to Jane who just smiled.

Maya stood up too and followed him towards the door. "I'm so sorry, mom was a bit harsh on you," she said when they were outside.

"I understand her feelings. She wants the best for you, and you can't blame her for that." Daniel smiled.

"I'll be at the bakery whenever you want to see me or we could meet after that," Maya suggested.

"I know, but I guess I'll be busy looking for a job," Daniel shrugged, "I'll see you soon." He kissed her on her cheeks, then took off. It seemed like he was in a hurry to get away from there and Maya understood why.

She went in and stood in front of Jane with her arms crossed. "Couldn't you be more polite? You scared him off," she said.

"I like him," Jane said, "He is a nice man."

Maya eased a bit. "Well, you could have said that to him," she said.

"I will next time." Jane smiled at her daughter.

Daniel was excited and full of enthusiasm for his new life. He had called David and told him everything, and then discussed on few matters. He had an explanation to give to Wendy too. She was very surprised to learn about him and Maya and was happy for them.

Daniel tried searching for a job similar to what he had been doing in Sydney, but later realized that this place was smaller compared to where he had been living. He had to start up with any work he could get. He had been travelling a few places and one day he was at the Cottesloe beach, observing the surfers and some men fishing on the pier. He missed going fishing with his uncle. There were a few fast food outlets near the beach front. He noticed a 'now hiring' sign in the window of a fish and chips spot. Daniel walked in and talked with the owner, who said they were looking for someone to work in the kitchen. Daniel took the job and it was fixed for him to work from the next day, which was a Friday.

When Daniel shared the news with Wendy, she gave her car keys to him and said that he could use it since she did not use it much. She used to walk to and from the café as it was not that far from her house. The next day, Daniel drove to work in Wendy's car. He had to work with the fryers, deep frying the fish and potato chips all day. It was very hot in there and he was sweating a lot. When his shift was over, he drove towards the bakery to see Maya. She was excited to see him and ran towards him as he entered. They kissed and hugged. Maya thought something was unusual.

"Are you okay?" she asked him.

"Don't mind me, I came straight from work," he grinned.

"So, you had been busy working huh," Maya said.

"Looking for one. Actually, just started today. It's at a fish and chips by the beach," he said.

So that explains the smell, Maya thought.

"I want you to come with me tomorrow. You relax by the beach during the day and I will join you later after work," Daniel said.

"Sounds great," Maya replied. She had no plans for Saturday.

After five, Daniel drove Maya to her home. She invited him in for coffee, but he refused to come in.

"I'll come to pick you up around twelve tomorrow. I start work at one," he said, and drove off. Maya knew that he was trying to avoid seeing her mother. She smiled to herself and went in.

Daniel picked her up after noon the next day. After dropping her off at the beach, he went to work. Maya strolled along the beach, played in the water and then laid down on the sand. Daniel returned from work and went straight in the water for a swim which made him feel fresh. He had brought along some fish and chips for the evening. They found a spot from where they could watch the sunset and settled down. They ate the food and talked while watching the waves. The sky was changing colors as the sun prepared to set, and the wind was getting cooler. Maya moved closer to Daniel and rested against his chest as he wrapped his arms around her and kissed her head. They watched the sun as it lowered towards the horizon. The view was beautiful.

"I love you," Daniel murmured, brushing her lips with his.

"And I love you," Maya whispered. It was the most wonderful evening she had ever spent.

From that day onwards, Daniel took Maya to the beach after work whenever she could manage. She got to learn to swim from him. One day, Maya invited him home for dinner, saying it was her mother who had actually invited him. Daniel was unsure, but when he went there, he found a nice ambience in the house and started to feel more comfortable around Jane, who was a different person that day. She was very cheerful and soft towards Daniel. They talked, ate and laughed throughout the evening and into the night. It was almost midnight when Daniel left.

Daniel continued to work at the place doing extra shifts whenever he got the chance so that he could make extra money. So far, he had been saving his income as he didn't have to pay for rent. When he was not working, he kept looking for another job and a place where he could live with Maya. David had suggested him to look for an old house which they could renovate later as it would cost him a lot cheaper. When he talked with Wendy about it, she said that there was an old house in the neighborhood, but it was in a bad shape.

Twenty-Three

Daniel stopped the car on a gravel roadway. Maya stepped out of the car and walked slowly towards the house as Daniel followed behind her. Dust blew on the driveway as their car drove through because it was not used for a long time. The grasses were long in the front lawn and around the house. Small wildflowers were blooming in the unkept garden. A hedge of untrimmed rosemary had grown over the windowsill in the front. The roof tiles looked intact from outside, but they wouldn't be surprised if it was leaking anywhere inside the house. The white paint on the fence around the porch was peeling off.

Daniel and Maya exchanged looks but didn't say anything. Daniel used the keys that he had gotten earlier to open the front door which squeaked due to the rusty hinges. The pungent damp smell hit their noses as they stepped into the living area.

Broken window blinds were dangling by a thread, showing off the cracks in the windowpanes. Spider webs could be seen in every corner of the walls which had damp patches on them. They were in a dire need for a fresh paint. There were three bedrooms in no better condition. The cooktop in the kitchen had stains all over it and was covered in dust. There was a small toilet and a bathroom with rusty taps, a broken sink and a dirty tub. There was a door from the laundry area opening into a backyard where stood a rotary clothes hoist amongst the tall grasses. Maya tried to rotate the line, but it wouldn't budge due to rust that had formed over the pole.

"There is a lot to be done if we want to take it," Daniel said as he raised his shoulders, eyeing Maya and trying to figure out what she was thinking.

"Yes, a lot." Maya sighed, then curled her arms around his waist. "But together, we can make a beautiful home out of it, our home," she beamed.

Daniel smiled. He was relieved that she was willing to take it. They kissed, standing in the backyard of their future home.

Daniel spent every hour, beside his work, in the house. He started by mowing the lawn with a lawn mower he had borrowed from Wendy. He found a lot of useful tools at Wendy's house and the rest he bought himself. He trimmed the rosemary bush in the front window and cleared the driveway.

When Maya came on her second visit, she said that it already looked much better. Together, they started to clean the house by scrubbing the floors. Maya dusted the windows and cleared the spider webs. Daniel scrubbed the peeling paint on the porch fence to make it ready for fresh paint. On another day, when Daniel was by himself, he worked on the plumbing in the kitchen and in the bathroom. He replaced the old rusty taps with new ones and checked the drainage. He carefully removed the broken and cracked windowpane and replaced with new glass. He got rid of the broken blinds and the rotary clothes hoist. He was thinking about putting up a straight clothesline but that had to wait.

Daniel had inspected the roof carefully and luckily it seemed to be in good condition. After days of hard work, the only thing remained to be done was painting and the final clean up. They chose a day when they both were available and started early in the morning. Both were wearing old pairs of jeans and old t-shirts. They spread newspapers all over the floor to avoid the paint drips. Daniel started to paint the ceiling with a roller and Maya took a brush to paint the porch fence. Around mid-day, they had lunch on the lawn. Maya had packed a picnic for the day. After lunch, they started again, painting the walls of the living and kitchen area. It was hard work but doing it together was fun.

Christmas was near, so Daniel wanted to finish the project soon. The following week, he came every so often to complete the remaining work. He finished painting all the rooms, put up new blinds on the windows, and then cleaned the house one final time.

After all the upgrades, painting and cleaning, the house looked as good as new, and ready for move in. Daniel couldn't move in right away though. The house was ready, but it was still empty without any furniture or utensils. They both had wanted to celebrate Christmas in their new home but that didn't seem possible this year.

Jane had talked to them, saying they did not have to rush with the move in and it was decided that they would celebrate Christmas eve at Maya's home. Wendy was also invited. Maya had invited Gloria too, but she had plans with Mark. They had a wonderful evening together, however Daniel was missing his uncle. David could not make it for Christmas as he had unfinished business to settle.

After dinner, Daniel and Maya carried their wine glasses to the back of the house and stood under the stars holding hands. The sky was clear and the weather was warm. Daniel wrapped his arm around Maya's shoulders and pulled her closer.

"Wasn't I lucky to find you?" he said, looking at the stars. He then looked down at her and smiled. "I love you," he said, and leaned down to kiss her.

"I love you too," Maya said before she closed his lips with hers.

Wendy and Daniel left late, around midnight. When Maya laid on her bed, she remembered Daniel saying he was lucky to find her. She thought she was the one who was lucky to find him. Growing up, she feared that she would never find anyone who would love her. Now it seemed like she was worried for nothing. She had found a perfect man who loved her so much. Or should she say, he had found her. He was the one who had made an effort to see her in the first place and now he had gone to extremes to be with her. There was a smile on her face when she dozed off.

Maya didn't see Daniel for the next few days. On the day before New Year's Eve, she found a note that was slid under the door of the bakery when she opened it in the morning. It was the first time she had found such a note and was intrigued by it. She picked it up and opened it to find out that it was from Daniel. She beamed as she read it.

Dear Maya,

We have a dinner date on New Year's Eve (tomorrow) at a special place that I discovered recently. I will pick you up in the evening at seven.

Love, Daniel

She was excited and wondered where they were going. It was her first dinner date ever. She pondered on what she should wear for the evening; she wanted to look special for him. She read the note a couple of more times throughout the day and every time she smiled as she did so.

The bakery was closed on New Year's Eve and New Year's Day, so Maya had all day to pamper herself. She chose a black asymmetrical ruffled midi dress which had a bodice and a fitted waist. The sleeves were short, and it had a low plunging neckline. It fitted her perfectly, clinging at her waist and the length just covering her knees. She had a pair of high heel straps to go with the dress. She spent more than an hour on her makeup and hair. She was spraying a hint of perfume on her wrist when Daniel pulled up in front of her house. Maya went to open the door before he could knock.

"Hi!" She smiled broadly at him.

"Hey! You are looking lovely," he said, admiring her, then extended his hand towards her. Maya held his hand and stepped out, closing the door behind her. Daniel led her to the car, opened the door for her, and she slid inside. He then closed the door and went around to get into the driver's seat. He turned to look at her and smiled. "Ready?" he asked her.

Maya nodded her head; the way Daniel looked at her gave her tingles.

"So where is this place you found?" Maya asked when they were driving.

"Oh, it's a beautiful place, I'm sure you will love it, but first we need to make a quick stop before we get there," Daniel said.

Where were they stopping? Maya thought, but didn't question further. She wondered what he had planned for the night. Whatever it was, she was certain that they were going to have a delightful evening together.

Daniel pulled the car over by the side of the road and got off. He came around to open the door for Maya who was still trying to figure out what he had on his mind because they had stopped near the Swan River. Daniel held her hand and led the way towards the riverbank. The place was alive with lights and decorations. Maya was thinking that Daniel might have chosen one of the restaurants by the riverside, but he didn't take her to any of them. Instead, he led her to a bench and made her sit on it, and then he sat next to her.

"I wanted to start the evening from the place where we started." He looked into her eyes as he spoke softly. "This isn't the place where we first met, but it is the place that gave me hope, where the magic happened." Maya remembered the day when she had met him sitting on that very bench, and she smiled sweetly.

"Close your eyes for a moment," Daniel said to her. She did as she was told. Daniel put his hand in his pocket and pulled out a gold chain. He put it around her neck and kissed her on her cheeks as he did so. Maya felt a cold sensation on her neck, she raised her hand to feel it, then opened her eyes and looked down below her chin. A beautiful pendent with an oval red stone was hanging on a gold chain. Ruby, she thought.

"It's lovely," she said, touching it with her fingers.

They sat there for some time. Daniel had his arm around her, and she was still holding the pendent between her fingers.

"I could spend the whole night here with you, but we have to get going," Daniel said.

"Okay," Maya smiled. She did not want to question anything, she just wanted to follow him and see what he had planned next. They got in the car and drove off. Maya was expecting him to drive towards some restaurants, but he took a different road. She was familiar with the road they were driving on and, in a few minutes, she realized where they were heading.

Daniel stopped the car in the driveway, in front of their new home.

Twenty-Four

All the lights in the house were on, giving the feeling that people already lived in there. They slowly walked, arm in arm, towards their house, admiring it in every way. It looked beautiful.

As they stepped onto the porch, Daniel looked at Maya and said, "And this is where the magic continues." He kissed her gently and then opened the door. They stepped in together, and Maya walked ahead as Daniel closed the door behind him. She did not know how to react; she wanted to cry and laugh with joy at the same time.

The house was still empty except there was a small table with two chairs set up in the dining area with a white linen covering the table. A bunch of red roses were blooming in a vase at the center of the table and a pair of white candles stood on either side of the vase.

Maya was still observing the view when Daniel pushed her gently from behind and led her to the table. He pulled out a chair and Maya sat on it. He stood behind her with his hands resting on her shoulders.

"I couldn't find a place more special than this," he said.

"This is more than perfect, nothing else could have been better than this," Maya touched his hands as she looked up at him.

Daniel smiled and went to open the refrigerator. He pulled out a chilled wine bottle, then grabbed two wine glasses from the counter top and went to sit on the chair opposite Maya. He lit the candles with a matchstick, then opened the bottle and poured the wine into the glasses. He raised one glass and leaned towards her. She took the glass with a wide grin on her face. Daniel then raised his glass and clinked it with Maya's, saying, "To us." They both took a sip and rested the glasses on the table.

"This is great, it's like a dream for me." Maya put her hand above her chest and touched the red stone dangling there. She smiled and said, "I knew it was going to be special, but I hadn't expected this, in our house. Thank you."

"It's my pleasure," Daniel said, feeling proud.

They took a few more sips of the wine, then Maya looked around, pretending to search for something. "So, what's for dinner?" she asked. She was trying to tease him.

"Oh yeah, wait a second." Daniel got up and went into the kitchen. Maya waited in anticipation, wondering what he could have prepared for them, especially with no utensils in the house. Daniel was back with two boxes of noodles.

"I hope it's still warm," he said, placing one box in front of Maya. She couldn't hold her giggle as she found it very amusing. "I'm sorry I couldn't prepare a fancy dinner, but I promise I'll make it up to you someday," he said, placing one hand on his chest.

Maya opened her box and started to eat, realizing how starved she was. "Hmm, this is good," she said with a mouthful of noodles, then gulped down some wine. "I wouldn't have wanted to go to any other fancy restaurant than this, I love it." Maya praised Daniel for the effort he had put into the evening.

They finished their noodles, and Daniel poured more wine into their glasses. They talked about the things they needed to buy for the house before they could move in.

"There is one more important thing to be done," Daniel said, pretending to remember something. Maya raised her shoulder slightly as if to ask what it was. Daniel felt his shirt pocket and then his pants as if searching for something.

"There it is," he said, slipping his hand in one of his pant pockets. He then pulled out a small box, and holding it in his hand, he stood up and walked towards Maya. He inhaled deeply as he knelt in front of her, then opened the box to reveal a ring with a small white stone on it.

"Maya, I want to spend my life with you. Please marry me," he said, looking into her moist eyes. She was trying to hold back her tears.

"But you already asked, and I said yes," Maya said.

"I wanted to do it the right way," Daniel explained.

"Yes," Maya nodded her head vigorously and extended her hand towards him. He slipped the ring on her ring finger.

He got up on his feet and so did Maya. They kissed and a tear rolled down Maya's cheek. The kiss was soft at first, then it got intense and passionate, both wanting for more and willing to give more. Maya had her fingers curled up in his hair, pulling him towards her. Daniel wrapped his one hand around her waist to hold her in his firm grip and the other hand was cupping her cheek. He moved his mouth towards her cheek, then ears, then lowered towards her throat. Maya moaned as she curved her body to lean backwards, raising her chest towards him. Daniel kissed her neck and made his way towards the plunge of her dress.

Maya gasped, the warm sensation of his lips sent shivers through her body. She pulled him towards her and kissed him intensely. Both were breathing heavily when they pulled away from each other. Maya touched his face, tracing his jaw, and then noticed the ring on her finger. She was overwhelmed again.

"So, when should we have the big day?" Daniel asked, as he played with her hair.

"Whenever you say," Maya replied, resting her head against his chest. Her eyes were closed and she was listening to the rhythm of his heartbeat.

"It might take a while to furnish the house to be ready to move in," Daniel said.

"Yeah," Maya whispered, her eyes still closed.

"How does mid-February sound to you?" he asked her.

"Great," she whispered again.

Daniel looked down at her and realized that the wine was a bit too much for her.

He shook her gently, "Let's take you out in the fresh air," he said. Then held her firmly by her waist and led her outside.

A cool breeze swept the hair away from her face when they were in the lawn. Her eyes were wide again and her mind began to clear.

"How are you feeling?" Daniel asked her.

"Good, why do you ask?" Maya looked innocent.

"No reason." Daniel smiled. "So, February is fine with you?" he asked again.

It took some time for Maya to process what he was asking. "Yeah, it's perfect." She clapped her hands with joy.

"Where should we have it? You might want to invite your family and friends." The excitement in his voice was obvious.

"We need to talk about that," Maya said, clearing her throat. The excitement in her voice was gone. Daniel waited for her to explain. "I don't want a big celebration. It will be just us and our families. And we will have it in the registry office." She was crisp. It wasn't a request. It was a statement.

Daniel was surprised. He had thought that she would have wanted a big celebration. "Are you sure?" he asked her.

"Yes, you have spent a lot for the house and we still need to buy things. What's important is that we are getting married. We can avoid the other expenses," Maya explained, and hoped that she was sounding convincing.

Daniel thought that she was right. "Okay then, as you wish." He smiled and hugged her.

Maya was quiet. She hadn't said the whole truth. She remembered Sophie's wedding day: the crowd, Sophie walking down the aisle holding her father's hand, and her conversation with her mother that night.

A faint cry of people shouting "Happy New Year!" could be heard in the distance. Daniel checked his watch which had struck twelve at midnight.

"Happy New Year, darling," he said.

"Happy New Year." She smiled as he leaned down to kiss her. They stood under the stars, kissing as they welcomed the new year and this new beginning in their lives.

Daniel dropped her home a little later. Maya quietly sneaked into the house. She did not want to wake her mother.

"Are you home?" Jane called. Maya could see the light in her room from underneath the door.

"Are you still awake?" Maya poked her head through the door into Jane's room.

"Couldn't sleep. How was your dinner?" Jane asked her as she signaled her to come inside. She was sitting on her bed, resting her head on a pillow with a book in her hand.

"Great!" Maya sounded dreamy.

Jane noticed the necklace on Maya's neck. "That looks beautiful," she said.

"Yes." Maya smiled and told her mother about the night.

"That was thoughtful of him," Jane said, when Maya told her that he took her to their house for dinner.

Jane was very delighted when Maya showed her the ring. "Wow!" she said, "Have you decided when?"

"He said mid-February," Maya replied.

"That means we have to start the preparations early." Jane sounded excited. "We need to pick a dress for you, book a place, send out invitations, and plan the party!"

Jane would have gone on and on with the list, but Maya interrupted her, saying, "Mom, we are not having a big wedding."

"Why do you say so?" Jane was surprised. All the excitement vanished from her voice.

"We have to save money, we still need to buy a lot of stuffs for the house," Maya said.

"I have some savings, we can use that," Jane protested.

"Mom it's not just about the money. Do you remember what I said after Sophie's wedding?" Maya's voice was distant.

"I thought you were over that by now," Jane said, almost in a whisper.

"Well, I'm not. I don't want it and Daniel is fine with it." Maya was stern.

Before Jane could say anything, Maya stood up. "I want to go sleep, good night, mom, and happy new year." She kissed Jane on her cheek and strode out of the room.

Jane kept staring at the closed door. She wanted to stop her and convince her, but she knew her daughter well. She wouldn't be able to change her mind.

Twenty-Five

David arrived in Perth a couple of weeks after the new year. Daniel was very happy to see him, and asked him why he had taken so long to come. David explained that he had made some changes in his plan. His initial plan was to sell his restaurant in Sydney and start a new one in Perth. Now he had decided not to sell his restaurant in Sydney. He would rather hire someone to keep it running while he started with a smaller one in Perth. So, it had taken him some time to find someone who could run the restaurant.

Daniel took David to his new house. Daniel had managed to fill in some furniture but there was a lot more needed. David said that he had got a very good deal and had done a great job with it. David was invited by Jane for lunch, where he got to meet her and Maya for the first time. They bonded instantly and felt like they had been family forever.

Through one of his regular customers, David had come to know about a small restaurant in Fremantle that had been closed by the owner due to financial trouble. He had been in touch with the owner and had finalized to buy the restaurant. In the following weeks, David was busy visiting the place, completing the paperwork, preparing to reopen the restaurant, and hiring new people to work there. Daniel would accompany him whenever he had time.

The restaurant was ready to open by the end of January. David invited Maya and Jane on the opening day. Wendy and Gloria were also invited. The restaurant was small and cozy, situated right on the wooden floorboards near the harbor. Everyone was enjoying the seafood and sweet wine when Maya pulled Daniel away from the crowd.

"Can we go see the big ships?" she requested.

"Let's go," Daniel said, and led her to the port.

One big ship was docked there, ready to leave the next day. Maya studied the enormous vessel, wondering what was so fascinating about it. Why had her father wanted to get on one of these and leave forever? She was lost, deep in her thoughts, forgetting for a moment that Daniel was with her. She had been quiet, hadn't even said a word as she kept staring at the ship with an expression on her face that he hadn't seen before.

"You okay?" Daniel asked, putting his arms around her shoulder. He knew she was thinking about her father.

"Yeah." Maya forced a smile and rested her head against his chest. "Please don't ever leave me." There was a quiver in her voice.

Daniel wrapped her in his arms. "I wouldn't survive a moment without you. I love you." His voice was deep.

"Why do you love me?" Maya asked.

"I feel wonderful when I am with you. I feel like I have purpose in my life. I feel alive and happy. You make me complete," he said, stroking her hair. He then pulled away to look at her, and asked with a sly smile, "Why do you love me?"

Maya lightened up and smiled broadly. "I think you cast a spell on me with your charms and now I cannot be without you." Then she added in a soft and serious tone, "My life has become more beautiful because of you, because of your love."

After visiting the registry office, they had booked the date for February 23rd which left them with only three weeks. Jane and Maya spent a couple of days finding the perfect dress for Maya. Jane had wanted Maya to wear a long dress that flared at the bottom so it would sweep the floor behind her, but Maya did not even try it. After a few looks around, she finally had her heart set on an ivory-colored, embroidered lace fitted dress that clung at her waist. It had a round neckline and short sheer sleeves with a length that just touched the floor. When she tried it on, Jane almost cried and said that she would be the most beautiful bride ever.

It was a week before the wedding day, and Daniel and Maya were busy arranging the furniture in their house. They had everything they needed, they just had to organize it all. When they were done moving things around, finding the perfect spot for every piece, the house looked cozy and very welcoming.

"Do you want to move in right away?" Daniel teased Maya.

"Let's make it more special, we move in on our wedding day after we become husband and wife," Maya tried to sound dramatic, clapping her hands.

"Ah, I can't wait." Daniel dropped onto the couch as he was a bit tired after all the hard work.

"Me too." Maya joined him on the sofa.

It was the wedding day, bright and shiny early in the morning. Wendy and Gloria were with Daniel in his house, helping him with the decorations. They put a couple of balloons and ribbons on the front door. There was a bouquet on the dining table and a bunch of red roses on their bed. Gloria used the paper ribbons to write Mr. and Mrs. on the wall of the living area. She even scattered a few flowers here and there.

"You should go get ready now," Wendy said to Daniel, who then went into his room to change.

When Gloria was satisfied with her job there, she took off to Maya's house. She would be driving Maya and Jane to the registry office later. When she got there, Maya was doing her makeup. Gloria helped her with her hair. When they were content with everything else, Maya finally slipped into her wedding dress. Gloria and Jane kept staring at her in admiration.

"Well, say something." Maya grinned at them.

"You are looking amazing." Gloria hugged her with extra care so as not to ruin anything.

"I'll go change now. We should get going soon." Jane went to her room. She would have cried if she stood there any longer.

"Oh! I need some final touches too," Gloria said, and went to put on some makeup.

Maya had noticed Jane was gone and went to find her. "Hey mom, are you ready?" she asked, as she entered Jane's room.

"Umm, yeah, almost." Jane cleared her throat, turning her back to Maya.

"You okay mom?" Maya asked softly.

"Yeah, I'm so happy for you, I got overwhelmed." She turned to look at her daughter and smiled.

"Let's get going. We don't want to keep the groom waiting," Gloria cried from the door in excitement.

Maya took a deep breath and shook her hands to shake off the nervousness. They got in Gloria's car and started towards the registry office. Daniel, Wendy and David were waiting in a room when they reached there.

When Maya entered the room Daniel stood up, looking at her in admiration. Maya went to stand beside him, he held her hand and squeezed a bit.

"You look lovely," he whispered in her ear.

"Thank you," she said, "You are looking wonderful yourself."

Just then a man in his late thirties entered the room and introduced himself, he was the civil marriage celebrant who would be performing their marriage. He asked if everyone was ready, then took a book from his table and held it in his hands. He asked Daniel and Maya to stand on his either side facing each other. They did as they were told, holding hands, gazing deep into one another's eyes. The others stood beside them, Jane and Gloria stood on Maya's side, David and Wendy stood on Daniel's side. The man started to read from his book saying why they were gathered there on that day.

He asked Daniel and Maya to say their vows.

Daniel held Maya's hand and looked into her eyes. "Maya, you are the best thing that ever happened to me. My love for you is one of the most magical feelings that I ever felt in my life. You make me happy and I want us to be happy together, forever," he said.

Maya's eyes had moistened, she took a deep breath and said, "Dear Daniel, your love changed the way I felt about myself. You make me feel special and beautiful. And I want to feel that way with you forever. I promise to be the best version of myself for you, for your happiness."

Everyone in the room smiled in admiration. The celebrant then explained the meaning of the ring and asked them to exchange their rings. Daniel put the wedding ring on Maya's finger and Maya put the ring on Daniel's finger.

He then said, "Now I pronounce you husband and wife, you may kiss the bride."

Daniel leaned towards Maya and kissed her, while the others cheered and clapped. They were asked to sign the register. The ceremony was over in less than an hour.

"To the newlyweds!" David raised his wine glass. Everyone cheered and clinked their glasses. They were standing around the dining table in Maya and Daniel's home. Maya was impressed by the decorations, and she thanked Gloria for her effort.

"That was the least I could do." Gloria winked at her.

They all had the food that David had arranged and a few drinks. They spent the afternoon talking and laughing. After some time, everyone said their good-byes to the beaming newlyweds, leaving them behind together in their new home.

"Hello, wife!" Daniel said, when the others had left.

"Hello, husband." Maya giggled.

They kissed while Daniel held her tight in his arms. Maya pulled away from him and went to the dining table to clear it.

"What are you doing?" Daniel asked, in disbelief.

"You have to know one thing about your wife, she does not like mess," Maya said, picking up the glasses.

"Then you surely don't want to mess your lovely dress." Daniel took the glasses from her hand and carried them over to the sink.

"Oh, yeah. I didn't think about it. I should go change," Maya said, wiping her hands.

"Yeah, you should and let me help you get out of it." Daniel swiftly lifted her up in his arms. Maya chuckled, wrapping her arms around his neck. He carried her into their bedroom, then laid her down on the bed.

"I thought we didn't want to mess my dress." Maya mocked him with a wide grin.

"We sure don't want to." Daniel pulled her up on her feet. He slid his hands towards her back, finding the zipper below her neck, he started to pull it gently downwards to her waist. Maya wiggled a bit, pressing her palms against his chest. Daniel then helped her free her hands from the sleeves. The dress plunged down, forming a pool around her feet. She stepped out of it, gracefully standing in front of him in her under garments, feeling a bit shy.

Daniel took his jacket off, watching her intently, then loosened his tie before pulling it over his head. He moved forward, then slid his fingertips from her elbows up to her neck. He removed the hairpins from her hair, letting it tumble over her shoulders, then moving the bunch to one side, he kissed her neck. Maya turned her head towards him, her lips searching for his. Kissing her lips softly, Daniel unhooked her bra and pulled it away revealing her soft breasts. He cupped them in his hands, pressing them gently.

Her heart raced, making her breathe heavily. She made her way through his shirt buttons. He helped her unbutton them and yanked the shirt off. Maya pressed her breasts against his bare chest. The feeling was sensational. Daniel could feel the heat from her breasts pierce through him. He moved towards the bed, taking small steps, leading Maya along, he then laid her on the bed. He got on top of her, pressing her legs with his. He moved a tangle of her hair away from her face and rubbed her lips gently with his thumb. Maya looked at him through half closed eyes, curled her lips into a smile and held his face in her palms.

Daniel gazed at her for a moment, then kissed her, savoring the softness of her lips. His one hand was on her head and the other one had found her breast. He moved slowly towards her neck, planting a kiss along his path. He moved further down, resting on the breast he was cupping with his hand. He kissed it, then sucked the nipple softly, sending electric spikes throughout her body as she moaned deeply. She arched her body to ease the tickles as he moved to the other breast. Taking his time there, he started his journey further down, kissing her flat stomach on his way. He looped his fingers through her panties and pulled it down through her slender legs and then freed himself from his remaining clothes. He positioned himself on top of her.

"Umm." Maya looked uncomfortable.

"Are you okay?" Daniel asked in a husky voice.

"I… umm… have to tell you something." Maya hesitated.

"Yeah?" He waited for her.

Maya was blushing by now. "Umm… it's my first time," she said in a whisper, avoiding his gaze.

Daniel smiled slowly, kissed her forehead and said, "Mine too."

Maya had never felt so relieved in her life, she beamed.

Twenty-Six

Daniel woke up when she stirred in his arms. He watched her sleep, she looked fresh and lovely even early in the morning. He smiled as he played with her hair. Her eyes fluttered and she opened them slowly to find him watching her.

"Good morning." She smiled and closed her eyes again.

"Good morning, darling." He kissed her nose.

"Hmmm…" she snuggled in his arms, squeezing her leg in between his legs. He slid his one hand down her back to her bottom and tugged her towards him. Her eyes widened instantly and with a wide grin, she dug her fingernails on his bottom.

"Ouch!" He pretended that it hurt. He grabbed her hands and pinned them above her head, then climbed on top of her. They made love one more time.

Both were out of breath, lying next to one another. With a satisfied smile on her lips, Maya closed her eyes once again. Within a minute, she was snoring lightly.

Daniel got out of bed quietly so as not to wake her up. He headed towards the bathroom for a morning shower.

After the shower, he went into the kitchen to prepare breakfast. He had stuffed the fridge the day before their marriage. He put the bread in the toaster, and took eggs, sausages and bacon from the fridge and started to cook. As the sausages and bacon started to sizzle on the pan, the aroma filled the house.

Maya felt for Daniel on her side with her eyes still closed, but he wasn't there. She was wide awake when the smell hit her nose. She smiled and stretched her body then got into Daniel's shirt that was tousled on the floor. Scratching her head, she went towards the kitchen to find him standing by the cooktop making eggs. She went and stood behind him, then slipped her arms around his waist, resting her head on his back.

"Hey, you are up," Daniel said.

"Hmm, it smells nice in here," Maya murmured.

"Breakfast will be served in a minute," he grinned.

"I should take a shower first." Maya turned away to go to the bathroom.

"That shirt suits you better," Daniel said, as he slapped her bottom lightly.

Maya jumped and ran away with a chuckle. When she was back, the table was set for the breakfast. There was toast with butter, scrambled eggs, sausages and bacon, and a steaming pot of coffee.

"This is so good," Maya said, with a mouthful. They had a hearty breakfast, chatting along, talking about the things they needed to do.

Daniel had suggested that they go on a trip to Sydney after their wedding, but Maya had said that they could go some other time. Right now, they needed to get a car of their own as they couldn't use Wendy's car forever. Daniel had agreed with her and they had got their first car after a few days.

After a month, Daniel came home one day and announced that he had got a job as an electrician in a company. Maya was very happy for him.

Every morning, they would leave home together to get to their work. In the evening, they would prepare dinner together, helping each other. A soft music would be playing in a corner and they would dance. Life was beautiful and they enjoyed every moment.

Daniel started to teach Maya to drive. She was frantic in the beginning, but Daniel trusted her and encouraged her. Within a month, she was driving without his assistance. When she was confident, she took her mother on a drive. Watching Jane getting excited in the passenger seat, Maya had never felt so proud of herself.

Three months into their marriage, one morning Maya woke up feeling unwell. She found the smell of food revolting and didn't feel like eating anything. She wanted to spend the day in bed. Daniel had to go to work, but on the way, he stopped at Jane's house to inform her about Maya being unwell. Later in the afternoon, Jane visited her daughter to find her curled up on the couch.

"What happened, darling? How are you feeling now?" Jane asked, resting her palm on Maya's forehead.

"I don't know, mom. I feel funny. Everything smells strange and I don't feel like eating," Maya said.

Jane looked relieved and smiled which surprised Maya. "Have you missed your period?" Jane asked.

"Well, yes. Why do you ask?" Maya was confused.

"Because you, my dear, are going to have a baby. You are pregnant!" Jane exclaimed.

"Really?" Maya asked, "Are you sure?"

Jane nodded her head in excitement.

Maya had mixed emotions: she was excited, happy and scared at the same time. One thing was for sure, the baby was going to bring great joy into their lives. She couldn't wait to share the news with Daniel. Jane left later in the afternoon after giving her some healthy food to eat. She had given her tons of advice on what to eat, and what to do and what not to do.

When Daniel reached home, he asked how she was feeling.

"I've got some news." Maya signaled him to sit next to her on the couch. When he was seated, she said, "You are going to be a father. We are having a baby."

Daniel was speechless for a moment, he then hugged her and kissed her. "Oh, I love you," he said, feeling emotional.

"I love you too," she said, holding him close. Maya had thought she would never be able to love anyone else except Daniel, but now she was already in love with the human that was growing inside her.

Her morning sickness got worse as the days progressed. She didn't feel like eating at all and when she did eat forcefully, she would throw up right away. Daniel did not allow her to go to work anymore. He wanted her to get enough rest and take care of herself. He would send her out on the lawn or backyard or lock her in the bedroom while he prepared dinner so that the smell wouldn't bother her much.

Her baby bump started to show slowly. Maya would stand in front of the mirror every day to look at her growing tummy. She felt the baby's kick for the first time and was very excited to feel the movement of life inside her. Daniel wanted to feel it too, but he had to wait for a week to feel it. Whenever he was off from his work, Daniel would take Maya for a walk. They would talk for hours about the baby, guessing whether they would have a girl or a boy and who would he or she resemble.

When Maya was alone, she would knit tiny socks, sweaters, hats and blankets for the baby. She was eight months into her pregnancy, and thought she looked huge. They had set up the second bedroom for the baby with a new crib and dresser filled with baby clothes.

Everyone was waiting excitedly for the day, but Maya was anxious and nervous. She had heard about the labor pains being very intense. Jane did her best to lighten her up by saying, "It lasts only for small time and when you hold the baby in your arms, you will forget the pain you went through in an instant."

Maya was in the first week of her ninth month when one afternoon, she leaked a gush of warm water. From what her doctor and mother had told her, she knew it was about time. They left for the hospital as soon as Daniel reached home from work. Her labor pains had started. They came in intervals and the intensity started to increase with each new one.

After an excruciating few hours, just before midnight, around eleven thirty, Maya gave birth to a beautiful baby girl. While she was still recovering from the pain, Daniel held the baby first. He couldn't stop his tears from rolling down his cheeks. He pressed a kiss on her forehead then held her close to his chest. He walked over to Maya and kissed her too.

"Thank you," he whispered, "She is perfect, just like you." Then he lowered the baby into Maya's arms.

Maya smiled and held her baby for the first time. Yes, Daniel was right, she was perfect, with soft light brown hair, beautiful brown eyes and lips that matched the color of Maya's pendent.

"Ruby!" she said, "We'll call her Ruby." She looked at Daniel, seeking for his approval and he nodded in agreement.

Maya fed Ruby and went to sleep as she was still tired. Daniel held his little girl in his arms and walked around the room to put her to sleep. He watched both his angels as they slept peacefully and thanked God for this wonderful blessing in his life.

Jane visited them the next day. Maya was feeling a lot better and the little one slept through most of the visit. Jane was overjoyed to see her granddaughter and waited impatiently for her to wake up so that she could cuddle her and play with her. Both Maya and baby were in good health, so they were allowed to go home the next day. Jane helped them settle in with the new member in the house. Uncle David visited them the following day, then Wendy and Gloria visited them the next day.

All of a sudden, they were very busy day and night. Maya felt like she could never get enough sleep, even though Daniel was up during the nights to look after Ruby. She would clean Ruby, feed her, change and then put her to sleep. Maya would then lay down to get some rest. She would have closed her eyes for five minutes and the little one's wail would wake her up. She did get annoyed for a moment but one look at her precious and she would forget how tired she was. Whenever Ruby saw Maya or Daniel's face, she would give the sweetest smile they had ever seen.

She grew fast and healthy with every passing day. She had started to move her hands and legs in the air, grasping firmly onto anything that her tiny hands could get a hold of. Daniel spent hours playing with her, crouching on his hands and knees while she was on floor. Her giggles filled the house. She would shriek to get their attention, inviting them to play with her. Looking over at her husband and daughter, Maya knew she was living the best days of her life.

Twenty-Seven

Ruby was eight months old and crawling all over the place. She put everything she found in her mouth, chewing on stuffs as she was cutting her first tooth. Maya had to be on guard at every moment, watching where she went, stopping her from pulling things. The only time she could get some rest was when Ruby had her naps or when Daniel was home playing with her.

One day, Daniel came home and told Maya that he had got a new job as a technician which paid him a lot more. Maya was happy with the news but then he added that he had to be away from home at times. He explained that he had got the job in one of the mining sites. He would have to be away for two weeks and then he would be home for the next two weeks. At first, the thought of him being away from home scared her. But then the money was good, and he would be gone for only two weeks. Maya thought she could manage.

Daniel was ready to leave for the first time, and it was very hard for both of them. He held Maya and Ruby in his arms for a long time.

Maya had thought she would miss Daniel every second but was surprised by how occupied she was with Ruby. It was only when she was lying in bed that she did miss him. She counted each day, hoping the two weeks would be over soon.

And when they were over, Daniel was home looking like a mess. He said he missed them terribly and that even while working he had thought of them constantly. Maya asked him how his work was, and he said it was good but didn't give much detail. He played with Ruby throughout the evening, laughing with her as she giggled.

At night, after Ruby was asleep, the two made love which started with soft caresses but soon escalated to be wild. The separation had fueled the hunger and desire for both of them, and they couldn't get enough of one another. They were wrapped in each other's arms fast asleep when Ruby's cry woke them up.

"I'll go check on her," Daniel offered, as he slipped out of the bed. Maya smiled and went back to sleep.

Two weeks passed by in a blink and it was time for Daniel to go to the site again. This routine continued for a few months, and they both started to get used to it though they missed each other terribly at times. It was harder for Daniel as he missed Ruby too. He felt that it was the time when he should be with her, as she had started to walk and say her first few words.

The demand from his work made him stay at the site for longer sometimes. There were times when he couldn't get home for a whole month and this disturbed Maya very much. She wouldn't talk to him properly when he came home after longer periods, but she couldn't stay mad forever. A few days of togetherness and she would forget how upset she was with him.

Things were going on just the same except that Ruby was growing fast. She had past her first birthday and was keeping Maya busier than ever.

It was late in the afternoon one day; the sun was still bright though it had started to descend to meet the horizon. There was a light breeze which made it perfect to be out in the open air. Ruby was playing on the lawn which was freshly cut by Daniel during his last visit home. Maya was keeping an eye on her.

They had been out for more than an hour when a car pulled over in front of their lawn. Maya went to hold Ruby's hand when she heard Gloria's excited voice calling out her name. She ran through the grass towards them, stretching her hands in front of her. She hugged Maya so tight that she almost ran out of breath.

"Oh God, I missed you girl. How are ya?" she cried.

Before Maya could say anything, she bent down and scooped up Ruby in her arms.

"Hi, precious," she said to her, and lifted her high up in the air. Ruby seemed confused at first but then she liked her instantly and started to babble. She tried to touch her face and pull her hair. Gloria looked at Maya as if she was studying her. "You look tired," she said, then turned to Ruby and said in a baby voice, "Are you giving a hard time to mamma?"

"Mamma," Ruby said, pointing at Maya with her tiny fingers.

Maya smiled. "She is as good as a baby can be," she said, "How about you though?"

"I'm doing great." Gloria winked at her with a mischievous smile. "Can we go inside? I need a drink." Gloria walked towards the house with Ruby in her arms. Maya followed behind, wondering what was going on in Gloria's life, and then she remembered her boyfriend.

"How is Mark?" she asked.

Gloria had already stepped inside the house. Either she didn't hear Maya, or she ignored her because there was no reply. She put Ruby down on the floor in the living area and went into the kitchen. She found beer in the fridge and grabbed one.

"Do you want one?" she asked Maya, who shook her head. Gloria took her bottle to the dining table and began to drink.

"How is he?" Maya asked again.

"Who?" Gloria said without looking at her.

"Mark," Maya said, gazing at her.

"He should be doing fine." Gloria began to drink more.

"What do you mean, he should be fine? Haven't you seen him lately?" Maya was confused.

"No." Gloria was blunt. Maya raised her eyebrows as she stared at her. "We are not together anymore," Gloria said simply, but Maya was surprised. She couldn't hide her astonishment and went to join her at the table, forgetting Ruby for a moment.

"What happened?" Maya found it hard to believe. They seemed to be so happy the last time she saw them together.

"There were things that we didn't agree upon and we thought it was better to part ways," Gloria said.

"Oh dear, I'm so sorry." Maya felt bad for her.

"Don't be, I'm with someone else." Gloria winked at Maya and then gulped down the rest of the beer.

Maya's eyes went wide, she stared at her in bewilderment. She couldn't even ask who this new man was in her life. Her mind was still flashing the images of Gloria and Mark at her.

"His name is William. He is amazing, everything I could ask for in a guy and more. He makes me happy," Gloria's voice was soft and low. "And he is great in bed," she said with a wide grin, squeezing Maya's hand.

"Gloria!" Maya said with a smile and turned around to look at Ruby as if to check that she hadn't heard her.

Gloria roared with laughter. "She won't understand!" she said. "He takes care of me too. He cooks for me and checks on me that I am eating well. I love it. He makes me feel special." Gloria smiled softly again.

Maya smiled too; she was happy for her.

They chatted for a little longer, talking about Ruby and Daniel. After a while, Gloria stood up and was ready to leave. She was excited to meet William later in the evening.

Twenty-Eight

After finishing her chores and putting Ruby to bed, Maya lay in her bed wide awake, pondering on things Gloria had said earlier that afternoon. She found it hard to accept that Gloria was out of one relationship and was with someone else. She wondered, how was it possible to not love someone you have been loving for so long? Would she ever fall out of love with Daniel? As soon as she had that thought, she was scared, she couldn't imagine not loving him. He had loved her when she had doubts about ever finding love in her life. She knew she could never stand another guy in her life, not even in her dreams.

Jane came to visit her another day and she looked a bit sad. When Maya asked what the matter was, Jane said that Mrs. Smith had passed away the other week. She had been ill for quite some time. Maya felt bad too. Mrs. Smith had always been wonderful to her when she went to her house with Jane. She remembered Sophie and asked how she was doing. Jane replied that she was doing good and that she had three kids now.

"Are you feeling okay, dear? You look tired." Jane was concerned, seeing Maya slumped on the couch.

"Ruby was up a few times last night. I didn't get to sleep properly," Maya said.

"It would have been easy for you if Daniel was here. You could take turns looking after her." Jane was worried about her daughter. "Do you want me to stay tonight? I will look after her so you can sleep well."

"Thanks mom, but it's okay. It's just sometimes she does that, otherwise she is a good baby." Maya smiled sweetly, looking at Ruby.

Yes, it would have been wonderful if Daniel was always home. But life was not always as you want it to be. Her mom had lived her life without knowing what it was like to be loved by her husband. Yet she always seemed to be calm and happy around her. Was she like that always or did she put up a different face when she was with her? She never knew. One thing she knew for sure was that her mother was a strong woman.

And she had to be strong too. Daniel was only away for a few weeks and would be coming home in between. He didn't like being away from home either, but he was doing it for them, for his family. She could support him by taking care of their home and their baby.

A couple of days later, Gloria stopped by her house. A handsome young man was standing behind her when Maya opened the door. Looking at Gloria's wide grin, she knew that he was William. Gloria hugged her tight and asked how she was doing. She then introduced them to one another.

"It's good to see you," William said to Maya with a smile, extending his right hand.

"I was looking forward to see you." Maya smiled back and shook his hand.

Maya noticed that he had strong jawbones and when he smiled, it lit up his brown eyes.

"He is handsome," Maya whispered into Gloria's ear, as they entered the house.

"She thinks you are handsome," Gloria said in a loud voice. Maya felt embarrassed and rolled her eyes at Gloria.

"And what do you think?" William pulled Gloria into his arms with a grin. Gloria threw her arms around his neck, "Hmm, now let me think," she teased him. Then they kissed as if they were the only people in the room. Both were grinning at each other when Gloria pulled away.

The three of them talked about different things, Gloria was the one talking the most, as usual. She was sitting close with William on the couch. He had one arm wrapped around her waist. Maya could see admiration for her in his eyes. Gloria had a big smile that never left her lips. They made a lovely and happy couple.

They left after about an hour. Gloria said that they should all have dinner together when Daniel was home, to which Maya had agreed.

It was a month now and Maya was anxiously waiting for Daniel to be home anytime soon. But her wait wasn't over until the following week. She watched him from across the dining table as they ate their dinner. He looked leaner than before, and his unkept hair was longer. She could even see thin lines on his forehead and under his eyes.

"Are you eating well at work, dear? You look so tired." There was worry in her voice.

Daniel looked up at her and smiled sweetly. "You are worrying for nothing, darling. It's just that I did night shifts the last few days. I am a bit tired but will be fine in a couple of days. I am looking forward to spending time with you and Ruby," he said.

Maya nodded her head, but she was still concerned. When they were done, Maya cleaned the kitchen while Daniel played with Ruby. She was running around all the time, pulling down whatever she could reach and get a hold of. Daniel was behind her, paying close attention, half the time scared that she would trip over or bump into something.

"She must keep you very busy. Where does she get that energy from?" Daniel raised his voice to Maya without taking his eyes off Ruby.

Maya didn't say anything, she just smiled, watching them run and play. It would be wonderful if every night were like this, she thought, and then went to join them. They played until Ruby tired herself to sleep.

"You must want to sleep early too, you need some rest," Maya whispered to Daniel. They were still in Ruby's room, watching her sleep peacefully.

"What I need is you." He pulled her close and nuzzled behind her ears. He inhaled deeply as if to breathe in her smell. "God, I missed you so much," he mumbled.

"Shhh...!" Maya put her index finger on her lips. She didn't want Ruby to wake up now. They tip-toed out of the room. Maya was expecting them to go to their bedroom, but Daniel pulled her towards the kitchen.

"How about a drink?" he said, then went to fill two glasses of wine.

They sat on the couch close to each other, and Daniel pulled her even closer. Maya put her feet up and curled against his chest, holding her drink with one hand. Resting her head on his chest, she could hear the rhythm of his heartbeat. She smiled as she looked up at him.

"What is it?" he asked, as he pecked on her nose.

She just shook her head and rested it back to where it was before.

"This feels good," she said, and took a sip of her wine.

"The wine?" Daniel teased her.

"No. This…" she said, then turned her head to press a kiss on his chest.

He smoothed her hair and asked if anything new had happened while he was away. Maya shook her head at first, and then remembered Gloria. She told him about her new boyfriend, William, and that they wanted to dine together someday. Daniel said it was a good idea.

He talked about his work for some time and then realized that he was boring her as she was yawning. They both had finished their drinks. He asked her if she wanted more, but she shook her head. Was it the wine or was she feeling sleepy? He couldn't tell, but her eyes looked moist and drowsy. He put away the glasses. She lay on the couch looking up at him, resting her head on his lap. He stroked her cheek and chin as they gazed into each other's eyes.

He lowered his head to find her soft lips that were eagerly waiting his. They kissed slow, eyes closed, exploring every corner of their mouths. He moved his hand down her neck into her blouse then curved his palm around her breast. Her soft nipple hardened when he pinched it between his thumb and finger. He traced his mouth towards it and when he found the nipple, he put it in his mouth and sucked gently. She moaned with delight, then arched her body to move her chest upwards inviting him for more.

He moved his mouth to another breast while his hand still worked on the same one. Maya inhaled deeply, her eyes still closed, it felt so good. She then opened her eyes to look at him. The sight of his tongue flickering around her nipple aroused her more.

Maya started to undo his pants, then freed him slowly. He was hard, and she smiled at him shyly. She slid onto the floor and pulled him down. She was wet and ready for him and couldn't wait any longer.

"I want you now," she said, as she laid down.

He removed her clothes swiftly and entered her. She arched her body with a deep moan. He held her tight and kissed her hard as he moved in and out of her. They reached their peak at the same time. Daniel rested his head on her chest as she ruffled his hair.

Their heavy breathing returned to normal slowly. They felt a little chill as the heat dissipated from their bodies. Daniel reached for a throw blanket from the couch and wrapped it around them. They held each other close and drifted off to a peaceful sleep on the floor of their living room.

Twenty-Nine

An aroma of strong coffee hit her nose as Maya woke up in the morning. She opened her eyes lazily to realize that she was sleeping in their bed. He must have carried her there in the night and she hadn't even noticed. She smiled to herself. Was it the wine or their love making that made her sleep so deep, she wondered? The memory of last night made her flush, and she wished Daniel was still in bed.

She got up and walked out of the room to find him. On her way to the kitchen, she peeked inside Ruby's room to check on her, and she was still sleeping. She stood quietly by the kitchen and watched Daniel cook. He was making something in a pan. He liked to cook and help in the kitchen. He turned around to see her standing there.

"Hey, beautiful." He smiled at her.

"Good morning." She smiled sweetly and went to hug him.

"Slept well?" he asked with a kiss on her forehead.

"Hmm." She nodded and kissed him on his lips.

They heard noise from Ruby's room.

"I'll go." Maya went to check on their daughter. Ruby was standing in the crib and calling out for her mom. She squealed in delight to see Maya and stretched her hands towards her. Maya picked her up and went to the kitchen. Daniel was setting up the table for breakfast.

"Let's go to the beach today, I miss it," Daniel said while eating. Maya liked the idea and nodded her head eagerly. They could swim and lay down in the sun while Ruby played in the sand.

They spent the next few days going to different places. They went to the beach a few times and to the riverside. They went to meet Jane one day and Uncle David another day. They went to meet Wendy too. Gloria was still working there and was delighted to see them. She showed her engagement ring to Maya, who screamed in excitement and hugged her. Gloria said that she would give all the details later. She even fixed up a dinner date for the four of them. It was decided that they would meet and have dinner in a local restaurant. She also suggested that they could go to a pub afterwards.

Maya had asked Jane to look after Ruby the night they were going out. She said she would try to return early as she had no intention to go to the pub. It was the first time she was leaving Ruby with someone else.

"You don't have to hurry yourself, dear, relax and have fun. I can be here all night. She will be fine." Jane assured her.

The four of them met in a small restaurant that was famous for steak. Everyone agreed to have steak and beer. Maya went for a glass of wine. Daniel and William bonded instantly and were chatting about different things.

William asked about Daniel's work. He said that he was interested in working in mines. Currently, he was driving delivery trucks.

Maya was excited to know when William had proposed to Gloria and when had they decided to get married.

"It was last week. I hadn't expected him to do that, but I loved it." She grinned as she looked at the ring on her finger. "But I am not in a hurry," she added.

"But I am," William said, "I want to make you mine forever." He smiled as he took her hand in his.

"I am yours, darling." Gloria kissed him lightly.

Gloria was eager to go to the pub as soon as they had finished their dinner. Maya was not quite sure, she hesitated. Daniel assured her that it was okay. Gloria wasn't going to listen to her anyway, so she gave in. It had been a long time since she had been to a pub.

When they reached there, everyone got their drinks, but Maya said she had enough already. They enjoyed the night with music playing in the background and people talking around them.

"I can't wait for you to get married and have kids. Ruby will have a play buddy then." Maya said to Gloria in the middle of their conversation.

"For that, darling, you will need to have another kid 'coz we aren't having any," Gloria said, looking at William who was busy chatting with Daniel. They were too far from the girls to hear them.

"Why do you say that?" Maya was surprised.

"You know me, I don't have that kind of patience. I don't think I can handle them well," Gloria shrugged.

"You will learn once you have them." Maya tried to point out that she had done it and was doing good.

"Well, I don't want to learn," Gloria said. "Besides, William is fine with it. We don't want to settle down for a family, we want to travel around the world. There is so much to see out there."

Before Maya could say anything further, Gloria said that she needed another drink and went to the bar.

It was well past midnight when Maya said to Daniel that they should leave. Gloria said that they were going to stay a bit longer. After saying their good-byes, Maya and Daniel started for their home. Daniel noticed that Maya was quiet for some reason all the way home. They found Jane and Ruby fast asleep in Ruby's room, so they went to their bedroom without waking them up.

"Are you okay, my dear?" Daniel asked when they were in bed after changing their clothes. Maya hadn't said a word yet; she seemed to be lost in some deep thoughts. "Is something bothering you?"

"Gloria said she doesn't want to have any kids." Maya still found it hard to believe. She told Daniel what Gloria had said to her. "How can someone not want to have kids?" she asked. She had expected Daniel to be surprised but he was calm.

"It's their life, their choice. They have a reason for not wanting to have children. It's better to not have kids than to have them and regret it later," he said, looking away.

Maya felt a pang in her heart. Was he referring to his parents? She thought it was better to drop the subject. "I had a good time." She tried to sound cheerful to divert his mind.

"Yeah, me too. Better get some sleep now." He kissed her goodnight and shut his eyes.

After a few more days, it was time for Daniel to go to the site again. "Where does the time fly when you are here?" Maya was near to tears.

"It will fly by just like that and I will be back in no time." Daniel hugged her tight.

And so it did, time flew by as Daniel made his trips back and forth from work. Ruby was almost two years old when one day Maya realized that she might be pregnant again and this time her mother didn't need to tell her. She knew the symptoms and was excited to share the news with Daniel.

He was overjoyed too but was concerned about Maya being by herself when he would be at the site. Maya assured him that she would be fine, she hadn't had the morning sickness like her first pregnancy and was grateful for that. Daniel said that he would manage to be home more frequently.

She was eight weeks into her pregnancy when one afternoon, Maya had painful cramps in her lower belly. The pain was so sharp that she had to lay down for a while. She felt a little better after resting for some time. She thought about calling her mom but when the pain subsided slowly, she forgot about it.

Having done the usual chores and put Ruby to sleep, Maya went to bed. Ruby used to sleep throughout the nights, so she didn't have to feed her during the nights anymore. Maya also slept well but she felt something was wrong as she woke up early the next morning.

She could feel warm and wet under the covers. She reached to feel her clothes and when she lifted her hand out, there was blood on her fingers. Her heart skipped a beat, and she threw the blanket off in one swift motion. She sat up to find her clothes and bedsheets drenched in her blood.

Thirty

"No, no, no!" Maya panicked. Bleeding during pregnancy is not a good thing for sure, she thought. She should have called her mom or went to see a doctor the other day when she had the cramp.

"Oh God, why?" She started to sob. What had she done wrong? She was eating well and having enough rest. They were so excited about having their second child. What was she going to tell Daniel?

She had no idea how long she sat on the bed crying. Finally, she got up to clean herself and change the blood-stained clothes.

Jane arrived soon after she called her. Maya was trying to feed Ruby who was staring at her with curious eyes.

"Oh, my darling," Jane said softly, as she hugged her daughter. Maya started to sob uncontrollably in her mother's arms. "I'll feed her, you lay down," Jane said, after soothing her for some time.

Maya sat on the couch, touching her belly with her hands. The cramps had returned, and she felt weak. She soothed her tummy, imagining she was soothing the baby she had lost. Until yesterday, she was thinking about different names for this baby. She was thinking about how Ruby would bond with her sister or brother. She was imagining how handful they both would be for her. But now, she felt empty, and her heart ached. Until yesterday, she was excited to meet this little human, and today, she was mourning its loss. Why wasn't her body able to keep it safe, she wondered and started to cry again.

Jane watched her silently. She thought it better to let her pain flow with the tears.

They went to see the doctor later in the day, who examined her and confirmed that she had miscarried. Maya looked at the doctor with puffed red eyes, searching for reasons. The doctor said that she couldn't tell for sure because there was nothing wrong with her. She explained that many women have miscarriages during the first three months of pregnancy. It didn't mean that they couldn't have another baby. She advised her to have enough rest for now.

Jane was staying overnight to look after Ruby so that Maya could rest. She had called Daniel to let him know and he had said that he would be there on the next available flight.

"What am I going to tell him, mom?" Maya's voice was almost a whisper. Jane was sitting on her bed beside her after putting Ruby to sleep.

"You didn't do anything wrong. You heard what the doctor said. You won't need to explain anything to Daniel because he'll understand." Jane soothed her by gently touching her hair. "Sleep now, my child, you need some rest." Maya dozed off after some time while Jane stayed up all night.

The next day wasn't any better. The pain was still there, and she was bleeding heavily. Maya stayed in bed while Jane fed Ruby and made some warm soup for her. She didn't feel like eating but Jane said she had to regain her strength.

Daniel was home after mid-day. He found her sitting up in bed, resting her head and staring at the wall. He rushed to take her in his arms, and she started to cry again. "I'm sorry," she sobbed, burying her head in his chest.

"Hey! Shh!" He rocked her gently. "It's not your fault."

She pulled away after some time to look at him. His eyes were moist and red. He kissed her on her forehead as he held her face in his hands. "How are you feeling now?" he asked, then he added, "I'm sorry I wasn't here for you." There was pain in his voice.

Maya shook her head and hugged him tight. They sat there in each other's embrace for a long time. Maya felt a lot better wrapped up in his arms. She felt safe, and he gave her strength to overcome the pain, physically and emotionally.

Daniel was by her side all the time for the rest of the day. Jane was still there to look after Ruby. Daniel said he would be home for a month this time.

Wendy and Gloria came over to see her the next day and said how sorry they were. Gloria was sad and quiet while she held Maya's hand. It seemed like she wanted to say something but couldn't find the right words. She hugged Maya and patted her back softly.

Wendy came back again the day after. This time, she was there with Uncle David, who hugged Maya but didn't say anything. He then went to talk with Daniel while Wendy sat with Maya and Ruby. They stayed for quite a long time and when they left, Maya noticed a faint smile on Daniel's face. He sat next to her to explain what he had been talking about with his uncle.

Maya was surprised to hear that Uncle David and Wendy were seeing each other. Daniel said that he was very happy for his uncle, who had been alone for the most part of his life. Though he rarely showed it, he was sad within as he missed his late wife. He was still in love with her.

Today, he saw a different side of his uncle; he seemed content and happy. Daniel had never expected him to ever be with anyone else, but now he was glad that David had found someone to share his life with.

Maya started to feel better with each passing day. There were no more pain and with enough rest, she was gaining her strength back.

Jane visited a few more times. Maya looked at her mother and studied her features. She noticed a lot of grey hairs, and fine lines on her face.

She remembered Wendy and wondered if her mother would ever be with another man again. She knew her well enough to know that it was never going to happen, and it hurt her to know that her mother was going to live alone for the rest of her life. Maya promised herself that she was going to be there for her mom, always.

The month passed and it was time for Daniel to go to the site. He had said that he could stay for another week, but Maya said he didn't have to. She seemed a bit different to Daniel. She used to cry every time he was leaving home, but this time she didn't.

"See you soon," she said as she hugged him.

Daniel held her a bit longer; he missed her already. "It hurts every time I leave you," he said softly.

Maya smiled sadly. "I know," was all she said.

Daniel stared at her for some time then left with a kiss on her forehead.

Maya realized it too; she didn't cry this time. She missed him too and it hurt her when he left, but something had changed within her. It wasn't that she loved him less or anything like that. A part of her had died with the baby she had lost. She couldn't decide if she wanted to be alone or be with someone. Sometimes she felt like she needed space and sometimes she yearned for a hug.

As time passed, Maya became quieter. The only time she laughed was when Ruby did something funny or said something in her own baby language. She was happy when Daniel was home but her childlike behavior with him at times were gone, and now she was serious most of the time.

Daniel was worried about her and he missed her innocence. He wondered, did he have anything to do with it? Was it because he was frequently away from home? He even tried to talk with her about it, but Maya ignored him, saying everything was fine. She even felt irritated with him at times.

Daniel thought that if they had another baby, Maya would be back to her old self. He wanted to know how she felt about it. He shared his thoughts with her one night, unsure how she would react. She nodded her head, and there was a twinkle in her eyes, a twinkle of hope, but at the same time, she was sad too. "What if…." she began to say, but she couldn't finish.

"It will be okay, the doctor said so." Daniel tried to sound positive. They made love that night with passion and this time there was a hope too, a hope to have their baby.

The hope vanished when Maya had her period after two weeks. A fear crept through her mind, a fear of not having another child. She kept thinking about the baby she never got to see, never got to hold. She felt sorry for herself.

Ruby was almost two now. Maya didn't want her to grow up alone like her, she wanted her to have brothers and sisters who would be friends for life.

They tried a couple more times when finally, their prayers were answered. Maya missed her period. She was anxious for a week, and then went to see her doctor to be sure. After the test, the doctor confirmed her pregnancy. She suggested her to be more careful this time. Maya couldn't wait to tell Daniel.

Thirty-One

Daniel was overjoyed when Maya told him the news. He was even more happy for her.

"How are you feeling?" He was concerned.

"I am okay," she replied. She had morning sickness, but it wasn't that bad. Just like the doctor, Daniel told her to be more careful.

I was careful before too, she thought, but didn't say it out loud.

Her morning sickness started to get worse. She felt terrible in the morning and even during the day she would throw up anything she ate, which made her feel sick and weak. Daniel was at the site, so she called her mom one day when she couldn't take it anymore. Jane said they should go see the doctor at once.

After examining her, the doctor said that things were okay for now, however, it would be best if Maya took bedrest for the first trimester and then they would see from there, depending on how she would do.

Maya was scared; she couldn't go through it again. She prayed every day that nothing wrong would happen this time.

Jane had informed Daniel. He talked with Maya and promised that he would be home soon.

Maya had been resting all day but couldn't stomach the food she ate. She looked pale and thin which wasn't a good sign and it worried Jane. She knew Maya would feel better if Daniel was there with her, and she wondered what was keeping him. She had thought that he would be home the next day when she called him.

Daniel was home after three days. He hugged Jane. "Thank you for taking care of her," he said.

Before she could say anything, he marched towards the bedroom to find Maya. Jane noticed a big luggage by the door which Daniel had brought along.

Maya was sleeping when Daniel came in, but she opened her eyes as he sat on the bed beside her. She wanted to hug him but was too weak to get up on her own.

"It's okay, I am here now," he said, patting her head. "And I am not leaving you again." He bent down to kiss her forehead.

Maya just stared at him, not knowing what he meant.

"Are you not going back to work?" Jane asked from the door. She had heard what Daniel had just said to Maya. Then she realized why he had taken more time to come home.

"I left the job. I want to be here for them," he said, without looking at her.

"I am here, I can look after her and Ruby," Jane said, as she walked in slowly.

"I know, Jane, and you know how much I appreciate it, but I don't want to feel sorry again. She needs her husband by her side and Ruby needs her dad." He was still looking at Maya who was in tears.

Jane knew not to say anymore, and she left the room with a smile on her lips.

"You didn't have to," Maya said in a weak voice.

"I had to. I want to take care of you, of our baby. We've lost one, we don't want to go through it again," his voice was almost a whisper. "I'd never be able to forgive myself if anything happened to you or the baby."

Maya rested her head on his chest and let the tears flow freely.

Daniel took care of her day and night. He made sure that she ate a little at a time even if she threw up. Maya was already half better with Daniel around the house. She started to gain strength and put on some weight. They visited the doctor frequently who was happy with her progress.

When Uncle David came to know about Daniel quitting his job, he said that he did the right thing as nothing was more important than his family. He even suggested that Daniel work in Wendy's café when he could, as it was close to his house. Wendy and David were going to extend the café to open for the dinning hours. Daniel thought it was a good idea and that he would talk with Maya about it.

Maya said if that was what he wanted to do then it was okay. Daniel started to work there once the café was opened for dinners. Sometimes he would work at the counter and sometimes he would be in the kitchen. He liked to cook different dishes. He realized that he enjoyed it more to work here than at the mines. Every so often, he would call home when he was at work to check on Maya. Both David and Wendy had said to him that he could go home whenever he needed to.

Maya was eight months into her pregnancy now; her tummy was so big that she could hardly walk without holding onto something for support. She needed more effort to do even the simplest of tasks. She was so grateful that Daniel was home with them. He prepared breakfast and lunch for them every morning. He fed both Ruby and her before he left for work. Every day, he told her to call him anytime if she needed him. In the evening, he would bring something from the café so that he didn't have to cook dinner at home.

One afternoon, Maya felt slight cramps in her belly, and she was alert at once. She thought it better to go to the hospital, not wanting to take any chances, and called Daniel at work. He came home within a few minutes.

Her cramps were getting severe and frequent as the evening passed by. They stayed in the hospital overnight, and it was only the following morning that she was taken into the delivery room.

Since everything went well, Maya was allowed to go home late in the afternoon. Feeling proud and happy, Maya and Daniel went home with their newborn babies. They had twins, a girl and a boy.

Thirty-Two

Maya named their baby girl Jenny after her mother. They named their baby boy Jordon. Both Daniel and Maya were busy all the time looking after the newborns. If one cried, the other one cried too. If one was hungry, the other one seemed to be hungry too. They squealed, laughed, cried and played together. The parents' joy was doubled and at the same time they were tired twice as much. By the end of the day, both Daniel and Maya would be exhausted, and their nights were just as busy.

As they grew up, Maya would compare them with Ruby all the time. She used to tell Daniel that Ruby was much easier to look after. He would say that it was because they were two now, but Maya insisted that these two had way more energy than Ruby.

Ruby was super excited to have a little brother and sister. She tried to take care of them as much as she could. Maya could tell that she had a soft heart; she would be an amazing big sister to her young siblings. Maya's heart would fill with pride and joy whenever she watched her three beautiful kids.

Maya got so busy with the kids that she lost count of the days, months, and years. Sometimes, she felt like she didn't have time for herself, but she didn't mind. She was happy looking after her kids. And her happiness only escalated as they grew up, and they grew up quick.

Ruby started her school when the twins were almost four years old and still at home with Maya. Daniel was working full time in the café as he was handling it all by himself these days because Wendy and David were busy preparing for their move.

They had decided to move to a town called Albany which was south of Perth. They had been there a few times on holiday and had fell in love with it. Wendy said that she had worked for a long time and now she wanted to rest and enjoy her life with David, who had agreed with her. To buy their new house, Wendy was selling her old house and David was selling his restaurants in Sydney and in Fremantle. They were going to let Daniel run Wendy's café in Perth city.

Maya would drop in at the café sometimes during the day with the twins but wouldn't stay for long as the kids were hard to handle in there. Maya wished she could help Daniel in the café, but it seemed impossible for now.

One day after visiting the café, she went to see her mother. It had been a long time since Jane had visited them. She would talk with Maya on the phone now and then, but always made excuses when she asked her to come over.

Maya was upset when she saw Jane, who looked very pale and thin. She was holding onto the walls when she came to open the door.

"Mom! Have you been sick?" Maya rushed to hold her. The twins ran into the house as soon as the door opened.

"Just a little, nothing to worry about, dear." Jane smiled weakly. Her voice was shaky and so were her legs.

"Oh, mom! Why didn't you call me?" Maya hugged her. She helped her into the bedroom which was in desperate need of some fresh air.

"Are you eating properly? Have you eaten anything at all?" Maya could feel her bones as she helped her into the bed.

She went to the kitchen to get her something to eat. The kitchen was stinking with used dishes in the sink and rubbish in the bin.

Maya's heart sank. She had promised to herself that she would take care of her mom and what had she done? She didn't even know that she had fallen sick. She knew what she had to do now. She called Daniel at once and asked him to come over with his car.

When Daniel arrived, she talked with him and he agreed with her at once. They went to Jane's room and helped her out of the bed.

"Let's go home, mom," Maya said to Jane.

Jane stared at her daughter. "What?" She didn't understand her.

"You are coming with us to our place so that we can look after you," Maya explained.

"No, I can't." Jane struggled to set herself free.

"Why not?" Maya asked her.

"I don't want to be a burden to you. You have a family to take care of," Jane said, shaking her head.

"You are our family too." Daniel took her hands in his as he spoke softly. "We are sorry we didn't ask you to come live with us before. You have been living alone since I took Maya away from you. If you don't want me to feel bad about it, then you are coming with us."

Jane was quiet as tears rolled down her cheeks. "Please, mom!" Maya said. Jane looked from her daughter to her son-in-law, then nodded her head.

"Help her into the car while I get some of her clothes," Maya said to Daniel. He walked her out of the house and settled her in the car. Then he went in to get the kids. When he was done, Maya came with a bag in her hand. She locked the main door and went to sit beside Daniel. After dropping them off at home, Daniel went back to the café.

Maya prepared one of the bedrooms for Jane. She moved the twins' stuff into Ruby's bedroom. When the twins were fed and were taking their daytime nap, Maya helped Jane clean herself and change into fresh clothes. She gave her some hot soup with bread. With her stomach full, Jane fell asleep and woke up only at dinner time.

Everyone was home, the kids were playing with Daniel while Maya was preparing dinner. Ruby was happy to know that her grandma was going to live with them from now on. Maya was happy too.

She was grateful to Daniel for being so understanding, and for his kind words to her mother. She tried to thank him when they were alone in their bedroom for what he had done.

"I know how much you love her and worry about her. And I love you. I would do anything to make you happy," he said.

"You have done so much for me. Sometimes I feel like I haven't done enough for you." There was a hint of guilt in her eyes.

"You have loved me and that is enough," Daniel said, as he hugged her.

"I love you more than you will ever know." She snuggled in his arms.

"I know," he said as he kissed her.

Jane started to get color in her cheeks and strength in her body within the first week of moving into her daughter's house. Maya looked after her and made sure that she ate properly.

A month had passed, and Jane was as good as her good old healthy self. One day, she told Maya that she should go back to her house.

"This is your house now, mom," Maya said to her.

"But, Maya, I cannot stay here forever," Jane insisted.

"Why not? Don't you like being with the kids?" Maya was stern.

"Of course! I do, I love them," Jane said.

"Then?" Maya raised her brows.

"The house, my work, my stuffs…" Jane tried to give a reason.

"Everything is taken care of. You are not working anymore, and I've brought your useful stuffs over," Maya said.

Jane sighed heavily, shaking her head. Maya gave her a warm hug.

"Do you know how happy I am that you are here now? Don't you want me to be happy, mom?" Maya spoke softly.

"Oh, darling!" Jane hugged her tight.

"And if you can look after the kids, I can help Daniel in the café," Maya said.

"Yes, of course." Jane held on to her daughter for a little longer.

From the week after, Maya started to go and work in the café. She would drop Ruby to school in the morning and then go to the café. In the afternoon, she would pick her up and go home with her. On Fridays and Saturdays, she would work in the evenings too as it would be busy during dinning hours. She would return home late with Daniel. Some nights the kids would be asleep, and some nights they would be up watching a movie with Jane. They closed the café on Sundays so that they could spend time together as a family.

Maya liked working in the café, and with Daniel around it was even better. It brought back the memories of her working there before. She missed Gloria very much, it had always been fun working with her.

"You might not have even noticed me then, but it was here that I saw you for the first time," Daniel said one day when they were having lunch.

"To be honest, I did notice you that day." Maya smiled, looking into his eyes.

"You did?" Daniel seemed surprised. "I'm so glad that I came with Uncle David from Sydney that time," he said, holding her hand.

"So am I." Maya smiled. She always thought herself to be very lucky that she had met him.

Thirty-Three

It had been a year since Wendy and David had moved to Albany. Whenever Daniel talked with him on the phone, he would ask him to come over with everyone and spend a few days at his place. That year, Daniel made arrangements for all of them to visit his uncle for Christmas. He closed the café for a week, rented a big car and headed for Albany two days before Christmas.

They hadn't been on a long drive with the kids before. Everyone was excited for their holiday and enjoyed the ride with a few stops for lunch and snacks. There were farms on either side of the road, and the kids were delighted to see cows and horses on the farms. They could see vineyards throughout their ride too. The air got cooler as they got closer to Albany. Daniel had to stop to read the map again when they got into the town.

"Are we there yet?" the twins shouted at once.

"Almost," Daniel said, and started towards his uncle's house. It was only a few minutes' drive before they reached there. Maya noticed a bay in front of the house where a few men were sitting on the rocks with their fishing rods.

Wendy and David came out of the house to welcome them.

"It's a beautiful house!" Maya said, as she hugged Wendy, who smiled broadly. They all walked towards the house, and Uncle David noticed that the twins were hiding behind Jane. He spoke loudly to make sure that they heard him.

"Daniel, I was planning to go fishing this evening. Would you like to come with me? I don't think anyone else would be interested…" He pretended to look around. The twins peeked from behind Jane with a wide grin on their faces.

"Are you guys interested?" David asked them. They came running towards him with laughter. They did go fishing that evening. The next day it was warm and nice, so everyone spent the day in the water at the bay. Maya enjoyed it so much, the sound of small waves lapping on the rocks and sand was very relaxing.

On another day, Uncle David took them around the city, stopping at a few beaches. It's a wonderful place to be, Maya thought, and to live here would be like living a dream. The beaches were so beautiful, clear and blue, and the weather was perfect, it even drizzled now and then during the day.

They had Christmas dinner in the evening, and the kids were excited to open their presents while the adults were happy to be able to spend the time together.

They spent one more day touring the city before returning to Perth the day after. Wendy and David said that they should visit every year, to which Daniel agreed. In the coming years, they went there on holidays, once every year. They tried camping once and after that, Ruby insisted that they camp every time. She loved it so much that even when they were at David's house, he had to set up small tents in the backyard for the kids.

Following year, the twins started their school. The room they had been sharing seemed to be too crowded for the three of them. One day, Maya asked Ruby if she would like to share her grandmother's room. Ruby was more than happy as the twins bugged her all the time.

Maya and Daniel were busy in the café most of the time. The city had changed over the years, new buildings were built, new shops were opened. Many restaurants and cafés appeared around them, but Wendy's café was even more busy than before.

It had been almost six years since David had moved to Albany. Every time he talked with Daniel, he used to say that he was very happy and was glad that he made the decision to move there with Wendy.

One Sunday morning, Daniel got a call from him. Maya was alarmed by the way Daniel responded. He was shaking his head and mumbling something that she couldn't understand. He was rubbing his forehead with his fingers as if to wipe away his sweat beads.

Maya went close to him and put her hand on his shoulder. Daniel kept saying he was very sorry in a small voice. He said he would be there very soon and put down the phone. Maya waited for him to tell her the news. Whatever it was, she knew it was not good. It seemed like

Daniel was finding it hard to say, he had his face buried in his hands.

Maya couldn't believe when he said that Wendy had passed away the other day. Last time she met her, she was healthy and lively. She couldn't have been ill, otherwise they would have known. Daniel said that she had a stroke, but David couldn't say much about it as he seemed to be in shock.

"I want to leave right away, he needs me," Daniel said to Maya.

"I'll go with you," Maya said.

"No, you need to be here with the kids. If you can manage, then go to the café. I might stay with him for a couple of days." He got up to get ready.

"I'll pack your clothes." Maya followed him into the bedroom to help him. Daniel left after lunch.

"Call me when you get there," Maya said as he started the car.

Maya kept thinking about David all day. He had lost his love for the second time, that must have been very hard. She was able to relate to his loss and suffering somehow. She had lost her unborn baby which broke her heart, and now there was an empty space in her heart which would never be filled again. Her dad had left her when she was very young but that didn't hurt her much, it had just made her angry. As time passed, it didn't even bother her anymore.

David had opened his heart again for someone after a long time. They were very happy together in their new home. It had only been a few years and now she was gone. Maya felt sad for him.

She was waiting for Daniel to call her when he got there but he called only the next morning and said that his uncle was in a bad shape when he had arrived. He couldn't accept that Wendy was gone, and he seemed fragile and scared at times. Daniel had never seen his uncle cry before, and now he cried quietly staring at a void.

Daniel didn't know how to comfort him, what was he going to say? That it was going to be okay? It didn't sound right. He stayed with him in the house, and prepared meals for him which he hardly touched. He couldn't leave him alone like that, so he had decided to stay with him for a week.

David got a hold of himself after a few days, and he started to talk with Daniel.

"Let's go fishing," he said all of a sudden, one evening.

Daniel didn't waste any time and went to grab the fishing rods. They walked to the bay near the house then walked along the pier. Each one prepared their own fishing rods and stood on the edge of the pier. The water was clam and it was quiet around them.

Uncle David spoke again as they waited for their catch. "Life is a mystery. You cannot predict what's going to happen in the next turn. I wasn't hoping or looking for someone in my life. Then we got along, and the feelings that were dead for so long stirred again. We were happy together, and now she is gone. I am alone, again." His voice was small and full of pain. He stared into the water as he spoke.

Daniel stared into the water too. He didn't say anything as he felt a lump in his throat hearing his uncle speak.

"You're doing good, son," David said, still staring ahead. "Cherish your love every day, you're lucky to have her."

Daniel thought about Maya and suddenly he missed her. They stayed on the pier for a long time; it had turned dark already. They were quiet for most of the time, Uncle David only said something now and then. David remembered the evenings they used to go fishing in Sydney. He was going to miss his uncle once he returned to Perth. More than that, he would be worried about him being alone.

Daniel asked him to come with him to Perth, but David assured him that he would be fine. He said he didn't want to leave their house as it had her memories.

Daniel returned to Perth with a heavy heart. He called David once a week to check on how he was doing. David said he went fishing everyday with other blokes in his neighborhood. He spent more time with the community members, getting involved in community works. And he said that he was enjoying it. Daniel was glad that his uncle was getting along well.

Thirty-Four

"How do I look, nana?" Maya heard Ruby's excited voice coming from her room. Maya was in the kitchen preparing dinner, and Daniel was watching television. It was a Sunday evening when everyone was home, except the twins who hardly stayed at home. When they were not at school, Jordon would be hanging out with his mates and Jenny would be busy with her girls' club.

Ruby had been getting ready since the afternoon. It was her first 'real date' as she kept saying. She said she wanted to look perfect and kept asking her grandmother how she looked every so often. Ruby had been with a couple of boys before, when she was in high school, but she had never been so anxious. She said she really liked this guy and hoped that they would have a great time together on their first date. She had mentioned him many times since she had met him. From her talks, he seemed to be a nice man and Maya hoped that he was.

Ruby was still in her room when there was a knock on the front door. Maya could hear a small cry from Ruby's room. Daniel went to open the door, and Maya tried to peek from the kitchen. They shook hands and Daniel showed him in. He walked in small steps behind Daniel. Before Maya could go talk to him, Ruby came out of her room.

"Hi!" she said in a sweet voice.

Everyone turned to look at her. She had a shy smile on her face and looked lovely in her purple dress. Jane was behind her feeling proud of her granddaughter.

"Mom, this is Mike." Ruby looked at Maya as she walked towards Mike. "And this is my family," she said to him.

"Hello! Hello!" Mike nodded his head to Maya and then to Jane. He seemed nervous around them. He was young and handsome. They made a lovely couple.

"Bye, everyone!" Ruby waved at them, then looped her arm through Mike's arm.

"It was nice meeting you all," Mike said in a shaky voice as they turned to walk towards the door.

"Have a lovely evening." Maya managed to say before they disappeared through the door.

Daniel had walked behind them to the door. He stood there for some time, watching his girl get into Mike's car and head off on her date. He then closed the door and went to watch the TV again. Jane went back to her room with a smile on her lips.

Ruby had just passed her eighteenth birthday and she had grown into a beautiful lady. Not only did she have beautiful features, she was kindhearted too. She was always calm and soft spoken. She had finished her studies and was working as a receptionist in an accounting firm.

She had met Mike when he had come to her office. He was an apprentice in a real estate agency. He visited her office a few times and once he asked her out for coffee. They both liked each other and enjoyed each other's company. After a few months, Mike had asked her out on a proper date. Ruby had been excited throughout the week.

When Maya saw Ruby today, she remembered her own date with Daniel, and how she was as excited then as Ruby was now. Where did all those years go? she thought. She walked towards the dining table, then saw her reflection in the mirror that was hanging on the wall above the table. There are those years, she thought when she saw the few grey hairs sprouting above her ears and the fine lines on her forehead. Unconsciously, she touched her grey hairs and sighed.

Daniel must have been watching her, "You look beautiful too," he said.

Maya was startled, and she turned to look at him. He was observing her with a sly smile. She went to sit beside him on the couch. "I don't give it a thought, but when I look into your eyes and see the way you look at me, I believe I am beautiful," she said.

Daniel tilted his head to one side as if to say 'really?' Maya raised her hand to touch his cheek, then noticed his grey hairs. "You don't look bad yourself," she said, touching his hairs. "We are getting old, Daniel." She smiled, raising her brows.

"What are you talking about? We are still young." Daniel pretended to get offended.

Maya chuckled. "Look at the kids, they are all grown up." Then she added with a dreamy voice, "Didn't she look pretty?"

He nodded his head. "She has taken her looks from you," he said, admiring her face.

"You know how to talk nicely to a lady, don't you?" She had a crooked smile on her lips.

"Why? You don't like it?" he sounded flirty.

"I do, when the lady is 'me'." She smiled broadly.

"Well, I had the experience of talking nicely to only one lady so far," he said as he pulled her close and kissed on her forehead.

"And I would like to be your last one." Her voice was deep. She rested her head on his shoulder. He kissed her again on her head, inhaling deeply. Maya knew in her heart that it was a silent promise he made to her, and to himself. The sound from the television was buzzing in the room, and Maya was staring at it, but wasn't watching.

She was thinking about herself and Daniel, how they had met, not the first time but the other time when she had seen him sitting on the bench by the riverside. She wondered what would have happened if she hadn't met him that day, would he have returned to Sydney and they would have never met again? Even the thought scared her, she shrugged a bit, but Daniel didn't notice.

She was lost in her thoughts again. The sweet truth of her life was that they had met, and he hadn't given up on her. He had done what he could, to be with her. She wouldn't have wanted to live her life any other way. She had a happy and loving family, and to her it was perfect.

Well almost, she thought, when she remembered her twins who were fifteen years old now.

They were taller than Ruby and very opposite to her in nature. They were loud, and always seemed to be busy with something. They were home only to eat and sleep. Now and then they complained about not having enough space in the house for them. When Maya tried to talk about them, Daniel would say that they were in their teenage years, and it was normal for them to behave that way.

After that evening, they saw Mike often. Maya invited him for lunch the following week, and Ruby went out with him for dinners almost every weekend. Everyone liked him, and Maya was surprised to see that even the twins enjoyed his company. He was like a part of the family within a few months. They had been dating for two years when one day, Ruby came home to announce that Mike had proposed to her. She showed her ring excitedly to everyone. All were happy for her. Maya was very happy for her girl until Ruby mentioned that she was moving in with Mike.

Maya tried to protest, saying she could wait until they get married, to which Daniel said that she was being unreasonable.

The day came when Ruby left the house to start a new chapter in her life.

"I'll miss you all," she cried, as she hugged each one. She felt sad to leave them but was excited at the same time. Maya knew who would miss her more than herself; it was Jane. She had been putting on a smile when Ruby was around, but as soon as she left, Maya found Jane crying silently in her room. She went to hug her mom, and both of them sat together feeling sad for a while. They knew the house wouldn't be same without Ruby.

The following year, Jenny said that she wanted to go to Sydney for her further studies. Maya tried to stop her, saying she could study here, but it was in vain. Jenny said she wanted to experience life in a big city.

A few months later, Jordon put forward his own plan. He was interested in photography, so he had decided to travel to beautiful places in different countries. Again, Maya tried to talk him out of the idea, saying he was too young to go live in a foreign country. Jordon just ignored her.

"Does anyone even listen to me in this house?" Maya said, feeling frustrated.

"I do," Daniel said with a smile. They were in their bed, the night before Jordon was leaving. Maya was too anxious to sleep. All of a sudden, their crowded house seemed to be too big for them. Maya sighed heavily but stayed quiet. Daniel put his arm around her. "In the end, it's just us dear, you and me," he said slowly.

"I can do with that." Maya smiled and gave a peck on his nose.

Jordon left the next day with a promise that he would call them every week and let them know where he was and how he was doing. He did call every week for the first few months while he was still in Australia. He seemed to be happy and enjoying what he was doing. Slowly though his calls reduced to once in a month.

Well, he called at least, Maya thought. Jenny never did. It was them who had to call and check on her. She would say she was fine, but she always seemed to be in a hurry. She would cut off the phone call, saying she was getting late for work or for a class. Maya was so grateful that Ruby was still in the same city and that she dropped by every now and then.

Ruby and Mike got married a year after their engagement. Even after trying for many times, Ruby had not been able to conceive. Later, they consulted a doctor and after IVF treatment they had their first child, a beautiful girl. They called her Mia. They had Josh four years after.

Uncle David visited them once or twice a year. One time, he suggested that Daniel move to Albany and open a restaurant there, now that all their kids had moved out. Daniel had said he would think about it but didn't really gave it a thought. His café was doing well in Perth. Maya didn't want to leave Perth either and her reason was that Ruby lived there. David once mentioned to Daniel that if anything happened to him, they could live in his house if they wanted to.

It was a few years after that talk when David fell ill. He hadn't mentioned it to Daniel at first, but when he was bed ridden, he told him about his health. Daniel left for Albany at once to look after him. Doctors had said that nothing was seriously wrong with David, but he had lost the passion for living. In spite of Daniel's relentless effort, after two weeks, David took his last breath.

Daniel was heartbroken. He didn't just lose his uncle, he lost his guardian, the person who had raised him and loved him. The person who had given him so much and taught him so many things about life. Daniel was going to miss him forever.

Time passed by and Maya had her usual routine every day. She and Daniel kept themselves busy in the café all day. At times, she would stay at home with Jane or she would babysit Mia and Josh whenever they needed her. They were wonderful kids who filled her heart with happiness. If she didn't get to see them in a week, she would drop by their place on the weekend.

The days were good, and she was happy, until that day, the day that changed the rest of her life.

Thirty-Five

It was the month of July. It had been raining for three days in a row. That day it was windy too; the tree branches swayed all day. Maya looked out of the window from inside the café but couldn't see anything. Daniel had suggested to close the café early and go home but Maya had insisted that they stay a little longer. Someone might come in for a hot meal in this weather, she had said.

She wished she had listened to him then. She wished they had returned home early and not waited for the sky to get darker, and the rain to get heavier. No one had showed up to the café anyway.

Maya had spent the evening walking back and forth from the window to the door, trying to sneak a peek through the curtain of rain, hoping to see someone walk up to them. Then she could tell Daniel, "See, I told you", but no one came, it was just the two of them. She looked over to him, and he wasn't even bothered, he was busy doing the calculations.

It rained harder, and the thunders were louder as the sky rumbled. Maya sighed heavily, and she debated in her mind if they should wait for the rain to get lighter. Then she thought, what if it didn't get any better and it rained the same throughout the night?

"Should we leave?" She had to raise her voice to make sure he heard her. He looked at her and nodded his head, then started to put away his logbooks. Maya went to the kitchen to check one more time.

"You wait by the door, I'll bring the car around," Daniel said, and left with an umbrella.

Maya waited by the door inside the café until their car pulled up on the road. She got out and quickly locked the door, then hurried into the car. She saw that Daniel was trying hard to look through the windshield, but even with the wipers in full swing, they couldn't see what was ahead of them. Daniel drove the car slowly. Maya looked on her side, but she could only see the rain. Their house wasn't very far from the café. It usually took only a few minutes in the car, but today it felt like it took forever. Maya wished to get home soon so she could get cozy in her bed.

They were approaching an intersection on the road, and Daniel slowed down even more. He proceeded with caution, looking on both sides of the road. Maya couldn't see any other car. It was just them. They were almost on the other side when they heard the screeching sound of the tires through the rain. Daniel looked around, trying to figure out which side the sound was coming from so that he could avoid it. He saw the lights from a car on Maya's side, and he tried to speed up his car, but it was too late.

The other car slammed right into theirs with a loud thud. Daniel panicked and tried to steer away but the car had lost control. It spun a few times before hitting the curb.

Maya felt a sharp pain all over her body and then it went numb and she couldn't move. She saw Daniel lumped forward on the steering wheel; blood was trickling down from his head. She cried out his name, but no sound escaped her throat. She tried to reach him, but her hand refused to move. Then it started to grow quiet around her and darker too. Her eyelids closed slowly despite her effort to keep them open. It was all quiet and dark and peaceful, and then she went into a deep sleep.

Her eyelids were shut tight. She was in a different world, and in a different time. The sound of wheels turning and then stopping made her come back. She opened her eyes slowly; a car had pulled up behind Ruby's car. She looked around; she was sitting there all by herself. The sun had hidden behind the hills, but it was not dark yet. However, it was much cooler now. In fact, she felt a little chill on her wrinkled cheeks. Mike got out from the car and waved good-bye to his friend, who then pulled out his car onto the road and drove off.

Mike walked towards her, waving his hand. "Why are you alone out here? Where is everyone?" he asked as he leaned down to hug her.

"They must be in the backyard," Maya said.

Just then the front door opened, and Ruby peeked from inside.

"Good thing you are here," she said when she saw Mike. "Come help me set the table, the kids are hungry. Come in, mom, it's getting chilly for you out here."

"Coming, my lady." Mike grinned at her, then turned towards Maya to help her. He grabbed the handles of the wheelchair she had been sitting on and slowly turned her to the side then pushed her towards the door.

Ruby opened it wide to let them in. Mike led Maya to the dining table and set her on one end. Maya saw a big bowl of freshly prepared salad on the table. "Did you make that?" she asked Ruby.

"Yes. And that chocolate cake looks yummy. The kids love your chocolate cake," Ruby said. She was setting the plates for everyone. "Can you get the drinks, please?" she asked Mike.

"Sure," said Mike, and went into the kitchen. He got juice for the kids and beer from the fridge. He grabbed a bottle of red wine and glasses from the cabinet.

"There are some baked vegetables by the stove that mom made earlier," Maya said to Ruby. "Can you go and tell her dinner is ready? She is resting in her room."

Ruby went to find her grandma, then led her to the dining table. Jane sat next to Maya.

There was a family picture, framed and hanging on the wall. Maya and Daniel were sitting in chairs, their kids were standing behind them, and all were smiling. Maya looked at the picture for a long time. "I wish they were here with us," she said in a soft voice.

Ruby saw that her mom was looking at the picture. "You know Jenny, she is as busy as always. Good thing is that Jordon said he will be here for Christmas night with Nicole." Ruby tried to cheer Maya up. Nicole was Jordon's girlfriend; they had been together for two years now. Jordon had returned home and taken over the café after the incident.

Maya's lips curved into a smile as she continued to look at the picture. Just then, Mia and Josh rushed in through the backdoor and sat down for the meal.

"Go wash your hands first," Ruby said to them. They went to the bathroom and were back in a minute. Mia sat next to Jane, and Josh sat next to his sister. Josh looked at the bowl of salad and said, "I am not eating that." He made a face.

Jane smiled at him. "What do you want then?" she asked sweetly.

"Sausages!" Josh screamed as he tapped his knife and fork on the table. "We want sausages!" Mia and Josh cried at the same time.

"Sausages coming right up." A deep voice said from the backyard. The kids chuckled as they watched the backdoor. Daniel walked in with a tray full of sausages and steaks and a wide grin on his face. He limped a little as he walked. He had been busy with the barbeque in the backyard.

"Those steaks look too good," Mike said as he took the tray from Daniel and set it on the table. Daniel beamed. He loved to barbeque and was proud of his cooking skills. He went to sit beside Maya who was smiling at him.

"Hungry, dear?" he asked her softly.

"Starving," she answered with wide eyes. Daniel grinned as he served her the best piece. Mike poured the drinks as Ruby filled the kids' plates with sausages and baked vegetables.

"You will get the cake only after you finish your plate," Ruby said. Josh made a face again and everyone laughed.

Maya cut a piece of meat on her plate and put it in her mouth. It was moist and tender, cooked perfectly just the way she liked. "Hmmm, it's good. Thank you," she said to Daniel.

"Anything for you, my dear." He smiled as he squeezed her hand lightly. Maya smiled back at him, and her eyes twinkled as she looked at him lovingly.

Mia had a shy smile on her lips as she watched her grandparents from across the table.

www.ingramcontent.com/pod-product-compliance
Lightning Source LLC
LaVergne TN
LVHW041629060526
838200LV00040B/1504